UMBELLIFERAE

Susan Yaremczuk

© Copyright 2005 Sue Yaremczuk
All rights reserved. No part of this publication may be reproduced, stored in a retrieval system, or transmitted, in any form or by any means, electronic, mechanical, photocopying, recording, or otherwise, without the written prior permission of the author.

Note for Librarians: A cataloguing record for this book is available from Library and Archives Canada at www.collectionscanada.ca/amicus/index-e.html
ISBN 1-4120-5832-5

Printed in Victoria, BC, Canada. Printed on paper with minimum 30% recycled fibre. Trafford's print shop runs on "green energy" from solar, wind and other environmentally-friendly power sources.

TRAFFORD
PUBLISHING

Offices in Canada, USA, Ireland and UK
This book was published *on-demand* in cooperation with Trafford Publishing. On-demand publishing is a unique process and service of making a book available for retail sale to the public taking advantage of on-demand manufacturing and Internet marketing. On-demand publishing includes promotions, retail sales, manufacturing, order fulfilment, accounting and collecting royalties on behalf of the author.

Book sales for North America and international:
Trafford Publishing, 6E–2333 Government St.,
Victoria, BC v8t 4p4 CANADA
phone 250 383 6864 (toll-free 1 888 232 4444)
fax 250 383 6804; email to orders@trafford.com

Book sales in Europe:
Trafford Publishing (UK) Ltd., Enterprise House, Wistaston Road Business Centre,
Wistaston Road, Crewe, Cheshire cw2 7rp UNITED KINGDOM
phone 01270 251 396 (local rate 0845 230 9601)
facsimile 01270 254 983; orders.uk@trafford.com

Order online at:
trafford.com/05-0732

10 9 8 7 6 5 4

AUTHOR'S NOTES

This is a work of fiction. Any resemblance to persons living or deceased is completely coincidental. I have taken the liberty of using the names of my great grandparents as the protagonists but their characters are imaginary and their story an invention of the mind. I am truly grateful to my husband Gene who did his own laundry and his own cooking while the book was in progress. The cover photo and author's picture were supplied by him. A huge thank you to my children: Christina my first proof reader, Peter who reiterated –publish, publish, Nicholas who introduced me to the white goddess, Tobias who has composed tunes to go with each of the poems and to Joel and Natasha for allowing Shadrach and Druscilla to fall in love.

Dedicated to my great grandparents
Shadrach and Druscilla Pynn
whose names inspired me to write this book

PROLOGUE

O filigree flower
rooted in rock.
Frequenting fields,
whispering wildly
"Come back from the flames
of the fiery furnace.
Home to the harbour,
where lace
will enfold you."

In the beginning, this is what I knew. I descended from the family "Pynn", an Irish brood that arrived in Newfoundland in the 1600's. Along with their entire worldly belongings they brought to their new country the myths and legends of their kin and an insatiable desire to be connected with both the natural and the supernatural. I inherited a mystical longing to be linked to the past. My voracious appetite for the uncanny and a need to separate truth from fiction, and at the same time mix fact with fable, led me to discover as much as I could about my forefathers.

With the exception of my father, the Pynns were all wild red heads, sobriquet- carrot topped. This was a mark of distinction and so too I believed was a person's given name. Baptismal titles single one out from anonymity; give an individual a past and a direction for the future. Having an enquiring mind, I've always liked to discover the meaning of names, the thread of nomenclature that weaves its way through family records and to find historical figures actual or fictitious who share the same names.

The name Anne, my name, comes from the Hebrew Hannah and means with favour or grace. Saint Anne is the patron saint of Grandparents. Her protection embraces sailors, seamen and travellers by water. She shows particular passion for old clothes and lace. Her patronage extends to pregnant women and women in labour. There is in fact a question as to how Saint Anne herself became pregnant. A controversy regarding the accuracy of an ancient legend about her pregnancy and concern of begetting children for fear of her husband's reaction still mystifies religious scholars to this day.

The name Druscilla, my mother's name, means strong branch.

In the Old Testament, Druscilla was the daughter of Herod Agrippa, a high priest of the Jewish faith. After two unsuccessful betrothals, she married Felix – a pagan Roman procurator. It is said that a child of Druscilla and Felix perished in the eruption of Vesuvius. There is a pure white butterfly called the Appias Druscilla.

The name Brigid, my grandmother's name, is of Irish origin meaning the exalted one. The goddess of flame, the Saint of healing and poetry; her attributes are light and inspiration. Her symbol is the white swan. She is endearingly known as 'Mary of the Gael'. Saint Brigid was raised in the house of her father Dubthach. One day a notable scholar came to ask for her hand. But Brigid would not marry. "I have consecrated my virginity to the Lord." She said. "But I will give you advice." And she told the scholar how he would find a beautiful maiden dwelling in a wood to the west of the house, a girl whom would make him an excellent wife. Brigid's kinsmen were angered by her refusal to marry and shouted, "That beautiful face of yours will be some man's one day." Brigid thereupon disfigured her own features, destroying her own beauty to prove her resolve never to wed.

The origin of the name Shadrach, 'child of the fiery furnace' is unknown.

Queen Anne's Lace or wild carrot descends from the family "Umbelliferae". The centre of each umbrel has a reddish, purple dot. One fable associated with the name of the plant describes Queen Anne of England pricking her finger while working on a piece of lace, staining the centre of the pattern with blood. This timeless, favourite lace motif became popular and is often used when crocheting shawls and mantels. Another thought is that the name of the flower comes from Saint Anne, the mother of the Virgin Mary and the patron saint of lace-makers. The seeds of the daucus carota or wild carrot have been used for centuries as a contraceptive, effective when taken orally, immediately after coitus. Conception is not prevented however if copulation takes place while lying upon the flower either real or crocheted. Pregnancy will undoubtedly occur. The flower has two aliases, Devil's Plague and Mother Die. There exists an old superstition that if the flower is brought into a house, then the mother of the home will die.

And so, as you have read, my name is Anne Pynn. My mother's name was Druscilla and my father Shadrach. My grandmother was Brigid. In this the year one thousand nine hundred and thirty, I am a mature woman nearing the mid-point of my years, with a child of my own. This is the story of how in my youth, my maiden years; I unearthed what I did not know.

CHAPTER 1

1918

THE BOX

Diaries, dreams
and death
slip out of opened
cartons,
containers
and
caskets.
Solving mysteries,
curing malaise.

I never met my father. In 1900, the year of my birth, he sailed away on a schooner named 'The Annie Belle' and "not at all, not at all" did he return. Everyone said that, "He was a wanderlust, preferring the rolling seas and salt spray on his face to solid ground beneath his feet." I was born just a few months after his departure in the secluded village of Harbour Grace on the East coast of Newfoundland. The harbour stretched like a long knitted sleeve inland for almost five miles. Inside the sleeve was a strapping arm that sent a massive fist, protruding out from the sleeve's cuff, into the land's interior grabbing the adventuresome and hauling them out to sea.

At the time of my arrival into the world, most of the inhabitants of the village were either Protestant or Catholic. A stigma attached to religion hovered over both denominations like a cloud. A cloud, which given the right wind could whip into a storm and cover the land with a darkened shroud. A cloud in contact with the right breeze, that could break into billowing puffs and cover the harbour with a shadowy veil. Many of the Protestants established themselves on the harbour's North side while the majority of Catholics took haven on the South shore. The Pynns had intermarried and intermingled. Some paid homage to the Catholic faith, while others swore allegiance to the Protestant beliefs. Pynn families sprawled from North to South taking residence wherever their hearts had led them. Some succumbed to the clutches of the giant fist, others stood firm on the ground where they established their homes.

I always assumed I was named after the ship that my father journeyed out to sea on. I discovered later this was not entirely true. In an attempt to satisfy both religious sides of the family my mother christened me Anne after Saint Anne, to please the Irish Catholics and she held the baptismal ceremony in the Methodist Church to pacify the Protestant members. Her own personal reasons for choosing that name she concealed in the pages of her journals.

My Aunt Charlotte, (my mother's older sister and the woman who eventually raised me), said: when referring to my father, "Shadrach Pynn was a scoundrel, a blackguard who left a delicate wife with child, in search of a fool's dream." Genteel Aunt Charlotte, devoted to God and my upbringing, a spinster who had never quite uncrossed her legs, had great difficulty dealing with the reality of my mother's confinement. To her, it would be an impropriety to say "pregnant". She had no difficulty however in moralizing when it came to the subject of my father. Secretly, I believed that the man she called "good for nothing" was indeed good and all that good entailed; kind, caring, thoughtful, dependable, loyal and virtuous. For after all, he was my father.

My mother Druscilla died when I was seven. Everyone told me "she had a weak heart and one day it just gave out." I knew deep within the cavity, the core of my being that it wasn't a weak heart but a broken one, which caused her demise. It could no longer endure the absence of her beloved soul mate. For all that I speculated about my father, I never fantasized about my mother. She lived, I knew her. I had her to myself for seven years. I had touched her and had breathed her scent. Night after night, I heard her cry out with alarming intensity for her lost husband. She is buried on a high cliff deep in Newfoundland soil. The face of her tombstone looks out to sea, still watching, still waiting for the rogues return.

It is a poor grave with only a flat rock marker, yet the inscription speaks words.

Druscilla Pynn
1880-1907
LOST HEART.

As a little girl, I would sit on a crag next to her burial bed looking across the harbour at Old Sow Point to the north, viewing Feather

Point to the south, watching the waves roll in and recede back out to sea. Often the huge swells would crash against the Haypook, the slate rock at the centre of the quay and then the 'white horses on the bay' would gallop towards land. My mother had oft recounted to me the fable of the Irish chieftain, who had drowned on the morning of his wedding and could ever after be seen riding a white stallion across the water, preceded by handsome maidens strewing white flowers in their wake. Sometimes my mother worried that her own, adored chieftain had also drowned. At other times she believed her husband would return to her in much the same fashion, cantering forth in the sunrise on a great white steed, hurdling the foam breakers toward land, carrying a sweet smelling bouquet, a spray of umbelliferae, an offering of passion and peace. I heard so many versions of this wild yearning that it was easy for me to confuse the ebb and tide of the surf with the home coming of my father. The docking of every ship aroused my imagination and I pictured him walking down the gang blank of a decorated brigantine, picking me up in his powerful arms, clutching me close and "never again, never again" letting me go.

    I realized early in my teens that this event was unlikely to occur and that "I" would have to find "Him". I became obsessed with the idea. Possessed with this one thought, it overshadowed everything else. It dominated my days and preoccupied my nights. It cut deep into the sinews of my soul. Illness befell me. My appetite dwindled, lethargy set in, I drifted into deep sleeps. Hag ridden, the nightmares attacked me. My chest was weighted down with what felt like the Haypook crushing my very bones. The breath was forced from my lungs and I gasped for life sustaining air. I had relentless visions of my father. Sometimes he appeared as a barbaric mad man, roaming unfamiliar paths, searching nooks and crannies, looking into far corners for something or someone. Often he loomed as an unrestrained beast hunting for asylum, for solace from something frightful. Frequently he emerged as an insane monster trying to escape from something horrible. Repeatedly he arose before me as an appalling grotesque figure trying to break free of punishing shackles and return to the little fishing village where he was born. When I awoke from these dreadful episodes I wandered listlessly about the house with a raging fever invading my body.

I was emotionally ravaged.

Over and over in the dim light of my room I heard someone asking, "What to do, what to do?" It was Aunt Charlotte pacing the creaking floorboards beseeching God to help me through my tribulation. Charlotte's concern only escalated my condition, as she hovered over me rubbing her hands and praying for my deliverance from iniquity. She believed that all illness was the consequence of wickedness and the resulting symptoms, a punishment sent from above.

Old Doc Noseworthy was consulted. The only physician within miles, he had been administering to local patients for years. With his white examining frock hanging loosely about his shoulders, he poked and prodded, pushing his knowledgeable fingers into the flesh of my puddock. Attached to his forehead was a queer apparatus with which he looked into my ears and down my throat. Pressing on either side of my kingcorn, insisting that I swallow, he announced to Charlotte: "no swelling here." He listened to my chest with what he called his stethoscope. The metallic dial was as frosty as a chunk of ice against my skin, sending icicle trembles down my limbs.

He pushed again on my abdomen, "Does it hurt here, or here?"

I shook my head.

Nothing hurt.

Didn't they realize the suffering was in my head? The aching pain of not knowing thumped and pounded inside my skull. The anguishing fatigue of waiting, and the ceaseless throbbing of the searching heart, erratically beat inside my chest. Didn't they realize that the only cure would be the appearance of my father before me, as a normal human being? Finally the kindly, elderly physician announced that there was nothing that he could put his finger on. He prescribed a tonic and specific instructions: "Now Charlotte lots of rest and home made soup for the gal, and she'll be as right as rain in no time at all, at all".

But I wasn't.

Dark shadows circled my eyes as I slipped into a strange, melancholic plight. Burning and delirious one day, shivering with chills the next. Charlotte bundled me up in bed where I continued to sink further into some unknown abyss. When the doctor's recommendations proved to no avail, stalwart Auntie decided to take matters into her own hands.

She sent for Brigid, my grandmother.

This was quite an astonishing measure, as rarely would my Aunt consult with my grandmother. Her worry about my illness and concern for my well-being overrode any cold hearted feelings that she held toward the old woman, who was known amongst the villagers to possess healing powers. Bridie as she was fondly called, arrived with her satchel of remedies or her bag of tricks as she referred to them. Shooing Charlotte from the room with a wave of her hand, she prepared to cure my afflicted body and remedy my unfortunate feeble state of mind. In my delirium, I almost expected her to mix a mysterious potion, something bitter and disgusting to the palate that would be difficult to swallow. In anticipation of this repugnant medicinal draught, my throat went into spasms and I began to retch. Calmly she took from her sack a candle, a thin white taper. Lighting and holding it in one hand, she placed the cool surface of the other hand on my brow and began to chant, "May this room be filled with light and life." A certain heat transmitted through my skin and into my veins. My sluggish blood flowed smoother. Then she placed in my hands, an old cardboard container. "Here." She said. "This is your mother's memory box, all that is left of her belongings. Perhaps if you spend some time looking these precious items over, you might begin to feel better, begin to get some strength back. I sense in the atmosphere around you that you need ties with your mother and your father." Continuing to move about the room with the candle, she crooned incantations in a language quite foreign to me. Creating a comforting aura about the space, she precipitated sleep. Not an ordinary sleep, but one so deep as to be called celestial. And in that sleep I had a vision, strange but true.

> *Closing in toward me was a wolf. An albino animal with shining amber eyes, moving stealthily across frozen crystallized tundra. Just as it was about to pounce upon its prey, a shimmering cloud encircled the beast and then evaporated, leaving in its place a white swan. Floating on a pond, the idyllic bird moved slowly forward stretching its long majestic neck in the direction of my outstretched hand. Before I could reach out and stroke its feathers, the waters began to churn creating a whirlpool effect and the swan was sucked beneath the surface. Ascending from the centre of the eddy was an enchanting female with a string of pearls about her neck, the blue waters of the pond rose up about her body to form the soft folds of a cerulean robe. Her long white hair swirled, blending into the swell of waves, while gleaming scales sparkled in her mermaids tail.*

How long I was asleep, I could not tell. What the dream meant I did not know. But when I awoke, I still clutched the box in my hands, the very one which Bridie had left behind. Tentatively I undid the tattered, green ribbon that had once tied up my mother's silken hair but was now wrapped around the shabby carton. Everything about the box steeped of mystery. I wondered if it had once served my mother as a piece of luggage, for it was just about that size and shape. The corners were crushed, the battered exterior buckled in the middle as though someone had pushed it into a space where it didn't fit; like under a bed or into a small drawer. As I pulled the frayed end, the ribbon fell away and with a little assistance the lid prised up. Gingerly and with much trepidation I lifted it off——

And so it came to be that I began a long journey into the past that would ultimately lead to Shadrach Pynn.

CHAPTER 2

1898

THE PHOTO

Enduring existing
likeness.
Black and white
contrasting
colour cameo.
Capturing
forever a moment.

My condition of despair provoked by a lost father and an unknown heritage slowly disappeared and recuperation to a healthy state gradually took place. Every day was an exciting adventure back in time, as each item retrieved from the box spoke to me of the past, of those who had gone before. From those articles I found my roots. Roots that coiled and twisted deep into Newfoundland soil. I found declarations of love, souvenirs of lives lived, and requiems for those dearly departed. My mother's memoirs encased in journals and my father's cherished correspondence all burst into existence, entangling me it seemed, with the roots that had sprung from the seeds of my Pynn ancestors. And all the while "calling me, calling me" was the conjured image of my father.

As fate would have it, on the very top of the box and lying on a virginal, crocheted shawl was his photograph. A daguerreotype, a tinplate quite small actually, nonetheless large enough to rattle when held by opposing corners. The noise unnerved me, as if the man himself was trying to speak. Sometimes frightening me, the reverberation was like that of a rattlesnake's tail. Sometimes amusing me, providing flashbacks of infancy with the shaking babble of a childhood toy. Sometimes I heard the buzz of humming or the echo of singing; calming and soulful with a definitive beat resounding in my ear. It was difficult to discern my father's features from the tin- type. I desperately wanted to create the real person; what he sounded like, how he lived and breathed, how he felt and what he ultimately believed. I was reluctant however to part with the precious image so that a photographer could make for me a print. Finally, I ventured out with the original. Skipping down Water Street, walking past the little rows of houses and abodes of our neighbours, I wanted to shout to their rooftops in elated abandon that in my hand I held my father. I wanted to rejoice with children playing in muddy yards and holler at mother's hanging Monday's laundry that my father was in my possession. Past the corner grocery store, "William Garland & Sons" I capered. It occurred to me that Mr. Will as he was want to be called might have been a friend of my Papa. He was just about the right age. By my calculations my father would be about thirty-eight.

"Should I go in?"

I prodded myself. "Show him the picture, ask if he recognizes the man whom I hold in my palm? Not yet." I resolved. Venturing further along the street, I passed Hampshire Cottage probably the oldest house in the area. This historic place was purported to have ghosts and I always liked to stare at the windows in hopes of catching a glimpse of one.

Deciding I must get on with my mission, I quickened my step beyond Ridley Hall with its great ballroom and forward to the photography studio of the highly regarded Augustus Parsons. Aunt Charlotte suggested him because he was a god-fearing, religious gentleman. She said, that he would handle the negative with due care and concern. Wherever he went, his artistic reputation preceded him. His enchantment with photography began when he was only ten years old, probably because his father, also a renowned photographer, had gained international recognition exhibiting in Europe. Into Augustus' antiquated shop that had been owned and operated by a Parsons since the early 1800's, I trundled with my cherished possession. I explained to him what I required.

"If you could just make a picture for me out of this, I would be forever grateful. I would, I would." I said.

Augustus scratched his beard, brushed his brow with the back of his hand and agreed upon my request to produce a black and white.

"It will take a while, perhaps ten days." He said, huskily.

I groaned.

"That is the time, that is the time, my dear," he whispered.

Somehow Augustus never talked out loud. Always his speech came out as though he had a bad case of laryngitis. Village folk said it was a result of all the chemicals he used in his developing studio. Auntie said, "It's a penance he bares for a sin, long past committed." "What sin was that?" I asked. But she bowed her head and repeated that he was a good man and deserved our prayers for the return of his voice.

Trusting this man with my most valuable and treasured worldly possession, I left my father and bade him farewell for a fortnight.

"Out the door with you, out the door." Fussed Augustus.

Walking home, I pondered my position in life at the age of eighteen. I had read about other young ladies 'coming out' or 'making their debut'. Their backgrounds of course were not remotely similar to mine. I was not what one would consider a normal adolescent. Not pretty, although fetching enough with untamed curly, carrot coloured tresses that bounced about my face with cocky abandon. I had inherited my mother's amber eyes, soft, milk white skin that blushed a deep rosy hue if caught in an embarrassing situation and a dainty mouth, with a thicker lower lip, which Aunt Charlotte claimed protruded more than it should. Pouting was not on her list of acceptable expressions. "You are not a princess, Anne Pynn, so pull in that royal chin." As far as I knew, my looks were not the envy of any of my female friends, nor did any male acquaintances ever appear to take a second glance. I thought I had a pleasing personality but on the other hand, who was there to delight or for that matter to socialize with? If ever I did meet someone and I brought them around, they would surely be frightened off by Charlotte going over them with her beady little eyes. And if that wasn't enough to intimidate them, they would most certainly be put off by her questioning examination of their character. Arriving home, I was hit with a tirade about being at loose ends. Wherever did Auntie get those ideas from?

"Where have you been?" She snapped with a sharp tongue.

"I took the photo of my father into Augustus, as you suggested."

"I didn't suggest that you take that photo anywhere, I remarked that Augustus is a good man, that is all. Once again you deviously solicited information from me and then manipulated it to suit your purpose."

"But Auntie!"

"Don't Auntie me. I must remind you that deceit and cunningness bear a close resemblance to lying. Lying is punishable by God himself. Furthermore you must stop milling about and try to occupy yourself with more fruitful endeavours than spending time on the contents of that ridiculous box. And please pay attention to the hour, you have a habit of being forever late."

There was never, never a way of pleasing that woman.

Dropping out of school for young women in those post war years was a common occurrence and so in that respect at least, I did fit the predictable teenage pattern. Aunt Charlotte claimed that "busy hands were trouble free" and insisted that I acquire a respectable job for myself. As for herself, Auntie had very busy hands indeed: but from what I could tell, they were certainly not trouble free! She did laundry and cleaned houses for a few of the wealthier families around the neighbourhood, who she loftily referred to as her clients. She was admittedly an excellent seamstress and was able to mend garments and add fashionable clothes to the wardrobes of those same customers. Too bad I hadn't inherited her tailoring talents, for finding employment proved not to be an easy task. Given that I had few skills and appreciating that there were many pursuits that Auntie would never put her stamp of approval on, made the job-hunting an even more difficult undertaking. To make matters even more complex, the small fishing community once known as Harbour de Grace and boasting a population of over five thousand in the year of my birth, was in the decline. A current census posted a little over 2600 residents with the average salary a pitiful $50 a month. A disastrous economy was due in part to a bank crash, which had hit the entire Island in 1884, causing many businesses in the town to close and never again to open their doors. There were some small industries left, including boot and shoemakers, blacksmiths, cabinet-makers, sail-makers, coopers and tinsmiths along with regular shopkeepers, who hungrily plied their wares on Water St. between Le Marchant Rd. and Victoria. It was to these places with prospective employment in mind, that I decided to venture out one bright Thursday morning two weeks later. At the same time I planned to pay Augustus a visit, in order to retrieve my dear father.

Both encounters that morning required a pleasing presentation; the meeting with my future employer, whoever he might be and with the old photographer. I donned my best navy serge with the scalloped, white, picot collar, fastened at the neck by a cameo. That brooch was my only piece of jewellery and I adored it. Set in a fine tracery of gold, the carved, female profile to me symbolized strength and prosperity. Silk stockings were simply unaffordable and so, slipping my bare feet into my patent, Sunday shoes, clasping my pocket book and with a broad brimmed, indigo, straw hat perched jauntily upon my head, I departed.

My first inclination was to go straight to Augustus for the picture, but all to aware that Aunt Charlotte would quiz me about my employment search, I decided to deal with that matter first by making a couple of stops along the way. The spinster Henrietta Pike ran a sweet shop, called "The Corner Confectionary." She was a gentle little lady with the sweetest nature to match her confections. Never could a body pass by her window without craving one of her special delicacies. That day, the trays displayed delicious looking pink petit fours, mouth-watering fruit and custard tarts, an assortment of fancy cookies and best of all, her amazing cream puffs. I hoped she might require someone to take orders or to wait behind the counter. I could picture myself in a starched white pinafore serving the customers who frequented the shop, ringing the tinkling doorbell that heralded their arrival. There was always a plate of fat oatmeal biscuits for the 'wee ones.' For me, offering those small treats to the children seemed like the most satisfying part of the work. Concluding that I would probably end up as an old maid just like Hettie, I figured the job would suit quite well. But alas, she had only just hired another only a few days previous. A small group of tables had been arranged in the back, where steaming pots of tea were served for those inclined to sit awhile and visit. For a penny Henrietta would read your tealeaves. That morning she offered me a cup just brewed and then captured my attention by reading the leaves and foretelling my hazy future.

"See these lines, this one is the mark of wealth, and this one of love and this of sadness. Oh! Anne Pynn, I foresee you will soon fall in love and you are most definitely going on a long journey. Perhaps the sadness will be an illness or a death of someone close but certainly someday, you are going to be rich." Tracing each line with her tiny forefinger, she threw back her head and laughed at her soothsaying. I smiled with disregard at her prophecies. Anyone with even a dash of intelligence knew each of these proclamations could come true for just about all and sundry. Draining my second cup, I bade her good morning, "Thanks Henrietta, I'll remember your predictions. I will, I will."

I moved along the bustling thoroughfare. It appeared that all the townsfolk were out and about. English, Irish, French and American descendants of the original settlers, socializing peacefully as they went about their daily toil. Ridley's emporium established in the 1820's by the family's patriarch, Mr. Thomas Ridley, who had been the first president of the Merchants Society, was my next stop. Operated by Thomas III, better known as Tommy Three, the place appeared in a state of utter confusion. On one wall an assortment of clocks were ticking the minutes away, chiming and bonging out the hours, each striking at different moments. Beneath them in unruly piles were men's long johns, undershirts and jockey shorts, together with women's knickers, corsets, pantaloons and petticoats. Immediately next to the underclothes were stacks of pots and pans, teakettles and cooking utensils, all tossed in a tasteless jumble with a colourful collection of crockery. Hanging overhead like giant cobwebs were fine imported linens, lace tablecloths with intricate openwork designs and suspended upside down, were hand painted French parasols, their cupola's filled with silk ribbons and satin scarves. In the next aisle, half way up a stepladder perched Tommy Three who was stacking brightly patterned bolts of fabric. Tommy, I reckoned, was in his mid fifties. A thin and wiry individual with an abundance of nervous energy, he fidgeted and fretted and had a distracting habit of constantly blinking. I enquired if there might be a position for me.

"Tommy Three, could you use an extra pair of hands to help stocking the shelves or to wait on customers? Would you be interested in hiring me for a few hours a week?" I hollered up the rungs to him.

"So sorry Annie." Was his reply.

Sadly nothing was available. Working with Tommy Three wasn't in my future.

"How is your Aunt fairing these days?" he enquired.

"She's well, thank you Tommy. Good bye then."

He waved to me from his roost up in the rafters. I liked Tommy Three. He was a simple man with a heart of gold, who would do anything for anyone. It was in his nature to help the elderly, tease the young ladies and play with the children. He was my idea of a good father figure.

One more enterprise along the way piqued my interest, that of P & P's Millinery. Owned and operated by two sisters; Phoebe was the designer and Prudence the creator. They used a variety of appealing materials to fabricate an amazing assemblage of charming bonnets, bewitching berets, fetching felts, lovely straws and delightful toques. Accessories and ornamentations were available too, such as buckles, beads, flower garlands, silk ribbons, ostrich plumes, an assortment of other feathers and even fully stuffed birds. I knew I would quite enjoy assisting the ladies of Harbour Grace in purchasing the perfect chapeau to adorn their pretty heads.

"Sisters, sisters, would you by any chance be looking for some extra help?"

They looked one upon the other. They had an uncanny, silent way of communicating with each other, that no one else was privy to. Although it seemed that no words passed between them, there was an unspoken message and at the same moment, they both nodded their heads.

"Oh yes, dear Anne, we would like you to assist us." They announced in unison.

They wanted me to work two afternoons a week. Monday and Thursday were quickly chosen as the two afternoons that I would work. The sisters needed some time to attend to their own business of banking, to go to the hairdresser and to do their grocery shopping. They liked to do everything together and if I worked for them for a few hours, on these two days then they would be free to escort each other to various activities of their choice. I was to commence the following week, promptly at one hour past midday. Happily I thanked them for this great opportunity and bade them farewell.

"Goodbye Phoebe, goodbye Prudence, I look forward to seeing you next Monday."

The most important errand of collecting my father was next on my agenda. Augustus had the effigy finished and waiting for me, safely enclosed in a white envelope, pressed between two pieces of cardboard. He whispered that he himself took the original and that some other pictures were taken at the same time.

"It is puzzling" he said, "Why no one ever came to retrieve these other snap shots taken some eighteen years ago. I do seem to recall that the young couple, that would be your mother and father, were involved in some family crisis at the time. But I don't believe that anyone ever told me exactly what it was. Perhaps there just wasn't enough money to pay for more than the one photo. I have taken the liberty of enclosing prints of all the pictures that were taken at the time. I hope that is to your liking my dear Anne."

I gave him a hug and produced some coins and a bill, which I placed on the counter as I tucked my valued parcel under my arm. I couldn't possibly have gone home and had Aunt Charlotte's curious eyes peering over my shoulder. Privacy was of the utmost importance when viewing the pictures. It was imperative to choose a place where I would feel close to my father. So, I walked down to the wharf to be amongst the fishermen, some of who might have known or been friends with the man in my hand. I remember that day as if it were yesterday. The sun was shimmering in an azure sky. A slight breeze drifted over the docks where the anglers were mending their nets and swabbing the gunnels of their brightly painted skiffs. In the ripple of the waves lapping against the pier could be seen the majestic silhouettes of the schooners moored in the quay with their bows pointing out to sea. A few peddlers pushed their carts over the rough wooden planks. Hawkers, they were shrilling out their wares mostly on the deaf ears of the men who made their living from the water's depths.

Finding myself a spot, on top of a giant winch whose brass rings had recently been polished so that the suns beams bounced off like lightening rays, I settled cross-legged in the middle of this king size knob. I felt like royalty, resembling a princess whose inner being was discharging electric shocks out into the world. Opening the envelope and retrieving the photo, I rested it gently on my lap positioned in such a manner that Shadrach stared up into my face. My eyes met his, somewhere between knees and shoulders, about at the level of my heart. And there he was! Not black and white really but a mixture of muted greys and browns mounted on a buff background with a tiny gold border. Gazing for what seemed an eternity, at the smoky mingle of sepia and tan; there emerged what truly was a handsome presence, with abundant wavy hair and deep-set eyes that surely emitted a tiny twinkle. His stance exuded a haughty swarthiness betraying him for the rapscallion that he was purported to be. Traditionally men wore double- breasted suits with matching vests to have their pictures taken back in those days. Not my father. He posed without even a jacket and with a collarless shirt that was unbuttoned at its rounded neck. It was a peasant looking affair with large swooping sleeves caught up at the wrists. His light coloured trousers were wide and flowing so that the whole effect made him appear as a large bird about to take flight. His hand rested on the arm of an ornate wicker chair. I loved that hand. A hand that could have been used in Michelangelo's painting the Creation of Adam. For like the hand in the artist's work, it was scarcely possible to put into words the feelings aroused by the beholder. It seemed like a current passed from the image of the hand out into the world assisting in some hallowed earth-shaking event. — A perfect hand, with long strong fingers, that reached out and stroked my cheek. A mighty hand, that clasped my own, small appendage with ever so slight paternal pressure. "Talk to me papa, tell me where you are and how to find you. Tell me what pressing event took you away from your beloved Druscilla and unborn child."

Dropping out of the envelope onto my lap were two more photos. My mother sitting in the same wicker chair, her flaxen hair scooped up on top of her head, braided into a coronet with a few tendrils escaping on her temples. A string of pearls was fastened around her neck; each bead, a perfect globe matching the one placed next to it. There was a sadness about her eyes. Eyes, which appeared to cast a dreamy look off into the distance, while her hands folded together in prayer beneath her chin were angled in such a way that just a glimpse could be caught of her wedding band. The second photo was that of a newborn babe. There was a familiarity about the face and yet I did not readily recognize myself. The infant, wrapped in a beautiful piece of fabric completely covering her limbs was ensconced on pillows. I was quite sure it was a girl, for there was a fragile nature about her features and what seemed to be very dark hair was peaking out from beneath a beribboned, feminine bonnet. That was a bit of a quandary, since my hair is red and would have appeared, I think, quite light in any photo. I deducted that it must have been the way the camera caught the flash. Stamped on the back of each picture were the name of the studio 'Parsons & Squires' and the date – 1898. That too was baffling, inexplicable really. I thought; it must have been an error, as I was not born until 1900. Augustus obviously was confused about when the shots were taken and had stamped the incorrect date on their reverse sides. Although as a rule, Augustus was not inclined to make such mistakes.

Aunt Charlotte never said anything in Shadrach's favour. Being the "god-fearing" spinster that she was, she often quoted from the bible to make a point. When referring to my father she cited from the book of Daniel:

> *"You O King have made a decree that every man who hears the sound of the horn, pipe, lyre, harp, bagpipe and every kind of music shall fall down and worship the golden image: and whoever does not fall down and worship shall be cast into a burning fiery furnace. Nebuchadnezzar was full of fury and ordered Shadrach, Meshach and Abednego be bound together in their mantles, tunics, hats and other garments and hurled into the scorching pit."*

I talked to the photo in front of me just as if my father were there in the flesh.

"Auntie firmly believes you were cast into a raging hot inferno for never having repented of your sins. But I know that, Shadrach Pynn of the contrite heart and humble spirit was protected by the angel of the Lord who came down into the blazing chamber and drove out the flames."

In the Old Testament Shadrach, Meshach and Abednego are delivered from the fire unharmed and promoted to a place of honour. It was my firm belief that in reality it was "I" who must rescue my father and venerate his name.

Back home, in Charlotte's house, I gave Shadrach a place of honour on the mantel, occasionally on the left, more often "seated on the right". Take from that what you will but remember I didn't frame him.

CHAPTER 3

1880

THE SHAWL

A Queenly Quest
curiously created
by hands
who hold your infancy.
Created
to lie upon
in radiant
rapture.

My first day of work was a pleasant one. The sisters prepared a lesson in hat jargon to assist my shop-keeping vocabulary. In my few hours of initiation I learned many things about "the chapeaux" as Prudence and Phoebe called them. A bonnet was usually brimless with chin ribbons. A cap fit tightly and snugly against the top of the head. A beret lay flat and was made of softer material without a brim. Snoods were chenille nets made to cover coils of hair at the back of the neck and Leghorns were made of straw with drooping brims called flats.

Outside the wind was whistling about the street corners. Small gusts rattled the pink shutters, banging them up against the white walls of the shop. Big gusts lifted the rosy roof shingles, flapping them like hundreds of lips mouthing soundless words. Bits of paper and dried leaves whirled across the road and came to rest at the foot of the shop door. It was a peculiar, autumn day, to purchase a hat when it might easily have blown right off anyone's head. However, two ladies from South Side had ventured out with just that purpose in mind. Cousins they were, gracing the inside of the shop to acquire hats for a wedding and my very first customers. The women had funny accents. They were Americans they told me and had married brothers who owned a shipping company established on the South shore. Both women primped and preened before the long oak framed mirror, one gloved hand to the hair and the other to a brightly rouged cheek, questioning each other's choices. Babbling, chattering, lipsticked compliments, hectored back and forth. Momentous decisions were made. A white, wide brimmed felt adorned one head with a swathe of lilac netting surrounding the crown and cascading down the back. While the in vogue

"Merry Widow" in lemon yellow satin complete with a cluster of fruit and buzzing bees was the other selection. The hats purchased, were wrapped in mounds of tissue and secured in containers like birds in a nest. The lady cousins happily departed with hatboxes swinging from black tasselled cords while the wind's flotsam and jetsam twirled and floated about their silk stocking feet. They hardly appeared to have a care in the world and I wondered what, if anything at all filled their heads. The two seemed so frivolous and free as I watched from the window while they cavorted like young colts making their way along the streets corridor. I must admit that I was tinged with a little green for want of their carefree attitudes. I heard Charlotte admonishing,

"Envy is inadmissible."

I prodded myself,

"Be gone, be gone."

At the end of the day my responsibility was to tidy and close the little enterprise. While diligently performing the task, my eye caught two framed covers from Harpers Bazaar, which the sisters had hung above a glass display case. Both were intriguing pictures from the Victorian era. The one, a Christmas issue of 1897, portrayed an elegantly clad lady in a velvet gown trimmed with lace and sable fur. Her hat was a soft velvet toque embellished with two long ostrich plumes, which were fastened with a rhinestone buckle. The other was a gloved damsel in a ruffled cape, her stiff brimmed hat decorated with a profusion of ribbons and flowers taken from an autumn 1894 issue. Tacked on the wall beside these two prints I discovered an article from Leslies Weekly February 11, 1897. I was compelled to read it.

The Tale of the Hat.

> The evolution of the hat is also the story of religion, manners and morals. Its origin lies in the roots of things. The relation of the hat to affairs – civil, military, and religious – is accounted for by the relation of the head to the rest of the body. Keeping on the hat as an assumption of superi-

ority springs from our innate ideas, since it is practiced by all peoples.

The Christian takes off his hat in homage. A Roman slave received a cap when set free. On Roman coins Liberty holds a cap in her hand. After Nero's death the people wore caps as the emblem of their emancipation. Gessler's cap gave freedom to Switzerland.

At the convocation of the King, nobles, and commoners, during the reign of Louis XVI, the nobles were permitted to remain covered, whereupon the third estate took off their hats. Seeing this, the King put on his hat, that the commoners should not have the air of equality with the nobles. When William Penn wished to conclude his treaty with the Indians he put on his broad brimmed hat, and the simple natives hesitated no longer, but with awe inscribed their marks.

The beginnings of hats are in the mists of ages. The first mention in literature is in the Bible, Daniel III, wherein is related how Shadrach, Meshach, and Abednego wore their hats into the fiery furnace.

Mesmerized by that brief synopsis of hat history, I couldn't help thinking about the eerie connection between hats and myself. It must have been fate, which brought me to the two sisters shop. Clearly I thought if my father wore a hat to his destiny, then providence brought me to this place. Since my illness and since Bridie had given me my mother's box, wooliness often reigned within my head. I found myself frequently confusing fact and fiction. Reality and myth became muddled. I questioned my ability to distinguish between truth and invention. I tended to interpret things that I read, conversations that I overheard and situations that I observed with an eye and ear in the past. The past, that belonged to my mother and father and to the contents of the box.

After sweeping the floors and dusting the countertops, the door was carefully locked and the key deposited in my handbag. I journeyed back up Water Street and home to the 'vital vessel' from which my inquisitiveness was fed and by bewilderment assuaged. I was a touch tired from my excursion and a bit shivery from the chilling blasts that crept behind me and blew through my cloak against my back. The winds of Harbour Grace are known to pierce through garments sending fingers of cold up the spine but my resulting quivers were partially in anticipation of the unknown behind my bedroom door and beneath the bed. Once in my room, I reached into the box for the soft white shawl. It was a splendid piece of handiwork with nine identical squares at its centre. Each square bordered by a pattern of nine flowers, each a perfect replica of the other. Wrapping it over my shoulders and around my arms and settling into an old cane rocking chair for a wee nap, exhaustion took hold and soon I drifted off…

I was dreaming.

Someone was dancing, someone naked, except for the shawl which swirled about a lithe young body.

Looking closer I saw that it was my mother leaping and prancing, her milk white hair flying about her face. Her arms raising and lowering like the fluttering filmy wings of a butterfly.

Dancing through flowers on the edge of a cliff.

Someone was watching, surely a man. But the mist from the sea was masking his face.

Dancing to music.

The shawl now caressing, now billowing out with the wind, now back to embrace the beauty which it covered. The sweet sounds of a harmonica emanating from the sole witness, enticed the dancer to draw near.

Dancing with provocative sway.

Druscilla beckoned me to come closer. She cupped her hand over my ear and murmured—

There are things that you really remember from childhood and then there are things you only remember having been told. Sometimes it is difficult to decipher which memory falls into which category. I only remark on this because I am positive I remember being touched by Shadrach when I was an infant. I am positive I remember seeing his eyes peering into mine, piercing into my soul. There was a longing from that moment on that went with me to my grave.

I also know what I was told. My mother died in childbirth. My father John Soper who was blind, carried me in his arms to the nearest house. The reason for this, being that I needed sustenance and John knew that a woman in that house was nursing a child. For almost a year the woman Brigid would put the two babies to her breast, the one her own son born out of wedlock and the other the infant daughter of blind John Soper.

Perhaps it is true that he sucked my fist as we lay side by side in the hand hewn wooden cradle, while Brigid tapped the rocker with her foot. It is true, that a bond, which grew between us, bound us so close that we were paralysed on our own, crippled without each other. Unable to function separately, as though some parts were missing but together producing a perfect performance, a perfect harmony, we flourished.

"Dance Druscilla, dance for me. Throw off your clothes, be free."

When was the first arousal? I cannot recall, perhaps it was always there. When did the longing, the yearning, become desire?

"Dance Druscilla, dance for me —what I am feeling is indescribable, the swaying, undulating movements of your body, I cannot bare it any longer."

Who is speaking, whose heart is beating faster?

Whose salty tears do I taste upon my lips?

Who is laughing, who is crying?

"Down Druscilla, down upon the coverlet of lace. Woven by these bare hands with flowers from the fields, the leaves and stems twisted together, entwined like the story of our lives.

Dream Druscilla, dream as we cross the border into the sanctity of heaven".

I woke up startled. I had slept into the morning. The room was quiet, not a note to be heard and no one was dancing. But the woven fabric about my shoulders, I realized had a story to tell. Lacy flowers joined with a few stitches made up what could have been a veil. Ah yes, the flowers, the same ones that my mother was dancing in. Pinned to the corner was a note, "crocheted by Brigid." Brigid my grandmother, Shadrach's mother. And then I was abruptly filled with the realization: Druscilla's surrogate mother. She was an old woman, often pronounced a hermit by local people, still living alone on Lady Lake, a few miles outside of town. Why was it I had never talked to her of my parents, never asked her questions about their lives? Was it because Charlotte had rules? Rules that included keeping a distance between Bridie and us. Reluctantly I had honoured her authority. Up until that moment when I held the note and the shawl in my hand I had feared disobeying her. A voice within spoke to me:

"You must go to her quickly, quickly."

With great haste I took the shawl and ran the entire distance. Suddenly I was struck with an acute anxiety, that when I reached her tiny cottage, she wouldn't be there. My one last opportunity to hear her story would have edged away. An overwhelming foreboding flooded my mind suggesting she might have slipped the bonds of earth and taken with her, part of my past. As I approached the shanty, a curl of smoke rose up from the chimney dispersing itself into the mantle of clouds, which hovered over the lake. Was that the knowledge I sought vanishing upward before my eyes, escaping from my grasp into oblivion? No it could not be. I raced past the old cistern; the ivy covered stone well, up the dilapidated porch steps through the rickety screen door and abruptly came to a halt. There she sat, alive, flourishing. I whispered to myself a quick prayer.

"Dear Lord, I thank you."

The townspeople referred to her as "the bride of the white hills" after her namesake. "She's a strange one, she is she is," they rumoured.

And strange to me too, she was then, as she spoke, "Ah yes, Annie, I knew you'd be coming and none too soon either."

She reached out and touched the shawl with her gnarled fingers and brushed its smoothness up against her cheek. Her rheumy eyes lit up with some far-away thought as she patted her knee indicating a desire for me to take repose at her feet. I dropped down beside her chair glancing about the primitive surroundings; the perfect abode for this eccentric harridan A plentiful array of pots sitting on the windowsills, sprouting a mixture of herbs gave the small living quarters a wonderful aroma. Tied bundles of basil, sage, rosemary and thyme hung alongside buds of garlic and bulbs of onions from the kitchen's ceiling beams. Worn cupboards suspended haphazardly over the well-used sink held a variety of cracked china and odd shaped glasses on one shelf. Above these sat several jars of canned fruits and vegetables just waiting to be opened and consumed. Inside a doorless, paint chipped cabinet, sat containers storing Brigid's elixirs, her herbal medicinal cures were lined up alphabetically each marked with tinted labels. A brightly checked cloth was pushed up and bunched along one end of the sturdy timber table while a rolling pin, baking tins and mixing bowls sat ready for use at the other end. Hooked scatter rugs made from a multitude of cast off rags decorated the floor about the hearth, from which hung a big black pot that bubbled with something deliciously pungent. High up on a crudely constructed brick shelf were candles in copper holders, tapers of light with arched handles, an oil lamp and a box of matches, orderly lined up and patiently waiting for dark. Four ladder- backed chairs which were assembled along one wall looked like soldiers in dress uniform with their plumped up red velvet cushions trimmed with gold braid. Totally out of character were these chairs, too bourgeoisie for the owner of this particular dwelling but perhaps placed there as reminders of some by gone days or hopeful, for a different kind of future. There was something soothing about the surroundings, a comfortable melange that moved the senses, stimulated sights and sounds, inspired one to touch soft textures and taste mysterious tinctures. The comforting ambience seeped unknowingly into the pores, calming the mind and relaxing the being.

"Tell me about my parents, tell me everything you know." I pleaded, as I sat propped by Bridie's feet in front of the fire where coppery flames licked away at the logs and a kaleidoscope of colour occasionally burst forth from the embers.

Fascinated I listened to her treasury of a tale.

As a young girl I was passed over. Unattractive because of the mottled, purple, birthmark almost completely covering the left side of my face, I failed to lure any young men in my direction. My only wish, my strongest desire, was to meet a handsome young male who would carry me off to some romantic place, make love to me and give me children. But it was not to be. I cooked and sewed and cleaned and kept a big garden, first for my parents and then for my brothers and sisters until I was well into my thirties. I was the oldest in a pack of nine, with one sister who was the youngest and seven brothers in between. The two of us girls were the book-ends holding up seven volumes of Pynns. Each in their turn, the seven boys grew up, acquired jobs, found wives, betrothed themselves, started their own little families and were happy. They didn't need Brigid any more, any more. My sister Delilah was everything I wasn't and had many beaus, many romances. A rich businessman from St. John's eventually swept her off her feet. They married and lived in what I considered a mansion with servants to draw a bath, serve the tea, clean the house and manicure the garden. I can honestly admit that I wasn't jealous of her lifestyle, her home or her belongings but I did covet that garden. The garden, which was the envy of the entire city I'm sure was not like the ordinary back yard variety that I was accustomed to attending to.

Then I found myself alone——————without my sister, without my brothers and I so wanted a child, someone of my own to love and cherish. I wanted a child so badly; I didn't care a tick how I would acquire the child or what anyone might think of any inappropriate actions I might take in the process. I assessed every possibility, considered, judged, and sized up all potential fathers for this child. Looks weren't that important but the prospective candidate must be kind, intelligent and already committed to some other relationship. This last requirement was the most crucial the most important, as I did not want to become involved with the father. I wanted only a child. When the choice was made, like a giant female spider, I instinctively spun my web. Caught in the silken strands of my plan, my prey produced the desired ransom for his release and deposited it safely into my protective cocoon. So my baby, my son was created. I crocheted this shawl, an intricate networking of threads just like the spiders web and when he was born gently placed him on it enfolding him in its beauty. And when I embraced his tiny being, holding him close to my heart the fibres of the shawl brushed up against my cheek and the ugly scar miraculously disappeared. My son was perfect. I worshipped him. He was my joy.

Then something unbelievable happened. Trusted into my care came the gift of a wee baby girl, so tiny, so fragile. She was without a mother to love and protect her, without a mother to keep her safe. For you see blind John Soper's wife was carried away by the angels, just as the infant Druscilla drew her first breath. He was frantic, desperate for the child's existence, all he wanted was for the babe to survive, so he brought her to me to feed and tend to. On that first day, I bathed her and nursed her and when her belly was full and she was satisfied, tenderly I placed her along side Shadrach, secure beside him beneath the warmth of this coverlet. From that day forward they were bound together, not only with the cloth but arms and legs entangled, blood cursing through their veins beating a single rhythm, hearts pulsing, throbbing as one and thoughts vibrating and blending between them.

They were two people with one soul, never to be separated.

Separation would only result in devastation.

They grew out of infancy into childhood.

They grew into precocious children who romped the dunes, paddling at the waters edge with glee. They grew into carefree urchins cloistered away from the rest of the world and its complications. The one was so fair, so predictable and angelic, the other dark and mysterious with the strength of a champion. Hand in hand they raced headlong, chasing down the pathways of time into adolescence: where fondness became infatuation and adoration burst into passion.

Bridie patted my head and began to sing:

> O Annie my child
> born with God's grace.
> Wrapped in the beauty
> of Queen Anne's lace
> Child of lovers
> who came to the dell,
> neither are left
> their story to tell.
>
> Lovers who spawned
> in fields of grace.
> Wrapped in the arms
> of a heavenly place.
> Raised by my hand
> these children together,
> nothing could part them.
> Soul mates forever.

Now you must know
That your mother and father
Wept tears of sorrow
At the death of their daughter
First child of lovers
Buried in white
Slipped away quietly
In the dark of night.

You were the favour
sent down from above.
A blessing, exploding
Out of their love,
out of their anguish
and out of despair.
Conceived on the flowers
a blossom so rare.

The song was finished. Brigid's eyes were filled with tears, brimming over and spilling down her wrinkled cheeks. So many questions manifested themselves, rising up in my throat and pouring out, but she told me she had nothing more to say.

"Go home Annie, go home. Read your mother's journals and your queries will be resolved, uncertainties will become certain and doubts doubtless. Go home Annie, the answers are in the telling. The solutions are in the pursuit."

I took her hand and for a moment held it in mine, energy was flowing from her to me. I felt, that some world-shaking event was about to occur. She reached into the pocket of her worn apron, retrieving a miniscule leather sack that was sewn shut at both ends.

"Some infants are born with a caul." She said.

"It is a membrane that covers the newborns head. It is believed to have special meanings and to carry supernatural or mysterious powers. Shadrach was born with a caul. It is enclosed in this pouch."

Placing it in the palm of my hand she warned, "It should never be opened or its magical force will escape. Keep it with you always."

Then calmly as though nothing at all unusual had happened, she took out her old battered dudeen and began to smoke, her thoughts swiftly evaporating into the air as quick, as quick as her eighty years had passed her by.

"Good bye my child, go find the truth, go find your father and tell him he has a daughter."

I walked home lingering along the path, thinking what a peculiar woman, this grandmother of mine was. Reclusive, isolated and yet so knowledgeable a woman who never married, gave birth to my father, fostered my mother and just moments ago handed down to me a legacy. My thoughts were all jumbled together. I tried to put them into some kind of perspective. I was dizzy with enlightenment but weighted with problems. And burdened with questions, heavy, dangerous questions.

Who was Shadrach's father?

Who was the dead child in the song?

And—what was the significance of the flowers, the ones in my dream, the ones in the song and those in the shawl?

Suddenly like a bolt out of nowhere, I realized I had left the shawl with Brigid.

Charlotte was furious. She could not believe I'd been gone so long without telling my whereabouts. Enraged that I'd left the shawl behind.

"That shawl," she warned "although it may seem like an heirloom, has a devilish way; it has a way of causing calamity to its possessor, believe me, I know. You are a foolish, foolish girl, the most irresponsible young woman. You leave me fretting for hours, wondering what on earth has become of you. Its that red Pynn hair, that Pynn impulsiveness, they're constantly getting you into trouble."

When her temper flared, she ranted and raved like a snorting bull, wringing her hands and tossing her head. She, charging forward in attempt to strike, I dodging the rushing attack like a toreador. The angrier she got, the louder she screamed. A diatribe of profanities was uttered with a vengeance. I was afraid she might have a seizure or some kind of apoplectic fit. Nothing would calm her, she strutted her displeasure until it ran its course.

"Get to your room, get to your room," she shrieked at the top of her lungs.

"I should never have allowed you to keep that blessed box. I'll live to regret it, I know I will, I know I will."

Silence prevailed.

Quickly I retreated and quietly closed the bedroom door. Would she start up again or was it finished, her demented assault?

Still silence.

I stayed in my room for a few hours, occasionally peaking out down the stairwell to see if the beast had been tamed. And there she sat quiescent, more miserable than mad and reading her bible, atoning no doubt for her savage behaviour. I knew that if I broke her self inflicted solitary confinement and went to her at that moment, that middle aged woman who soon would be fifty, would apologize. I would be sorry that I had caused her distress and once again, we would be friends. Moments passed. A wave of humility washed over me. I was about to utter my regret when, suddenly, there was a great commotion at the front entrance.

"Missy Pynn, Missy Pynn, Miss Soper!" It was Tommy Three jumping up and down in great agitation, his boots clattering on the wooden stoop. Before either of us could attempt to answer, he clamoured down the steps, with shirt- tails flying he dashed around to the back bellowing, "Miss Charlotte, Miss Anne! Where in heavens are you too?"

We reached the foyer in tandem. Tommy Three all out of breath was panting and puffing, perspiring profusely, mopping up the sweat with a wrinkled handkerchief, flapping his hands about his flushed face in great consternation.

"Bridie is dead. Bridie is dead," he stammered, not realizing that he was blaring the words in our ears.

"Its that dreadful Mother Die," shouted Charlotte, just as loud, in a piercing, hysterical voice, grasping the door frame for support. "I told you, I told you." She cried.

A searing pain ripped into my chest. Had I been the cause of this ill-fated news? Panic clutched at my heart, the room spun dizzily about me and I collapsed in a faint onto the floor.

CHAPTER 4

1918

THE FUNERAL

Soothsayers speak
as prayers parade
extolling praise.
While coffins consume
the fortune and fate
of the one entombed.

On the day of the funeral, sun spilled in through the stained glass windows, which acted as a prism diffusing coloured shafts of light onto the hardwood floor of the little church. Dancing fragments of red, yellow, blue and green dappled the shiny, waxed planks. The antiquated organ wheezed out the notes of Amazing Grace. Aunt Charlotte and I sat in the front row of pews along with a few other relatives, most of whom I had never seen before. Charlotte was quiet, thoughtful, her ringless fingers folded in her black lap. Her head bent and her body humped inside a drab, grey, mended coat. Behind us, many of the townsfolk gathered to pay their last respects. Bridie was laid out in a simple pine box lined with white muslin, while tucked about her mortal remains were a few of the wild posies, which she so adored. The shawl was draped over the foot of the coffin. Desperately I tried to contain my emotions breathing slowly in and out, in an out, so as not to burst into tears or worse still, to pass out and keel over as I had the day before. I ventured a quick glimpse at the corpse, afraid of what I would discover as this was my first exposure to a dead body.

But – she slept.

Peacefully, with eyes closed, a long, auburn and grey plait trailed over her bosom, ending where her hands clasped together around her old, clay pipe.

Resting silently. Breathing in and out, in and out.

The Reverend Sweetapple read from Psalm 15:

> *O Lord, who may lodge in thy tabernacle?*
> *Who may dwell on thy holy mountain?*
> *The man of blameless life, who does what is right*
> *And speaks the truth from his heart;*

Who has no malice on his tongue,
Who never wrongs a friend
And tells no tales against his neighbour;
The man who shows his scorn for the worthless
And honours all who fear the Lord;
who swears to his own hurt and does not retract;

Sweetapple swayed, and then sat hunched on the altar bench, his slightly rounded shoulders about to cave in on themselves. His long, black vestments obviously made for a more robust stature hung loosely on his thin, bony frame. For a moment he could not continue. He seemed to be encompassed by desolation. There was an indescribable sadness about his eyes. He was an old man, perhaps as old as my Grandmother. It was clear he was overcome with emotion and for a fleeting second his faith seemed to falter. He ran his fingers through his thin white hair and somehow mustered enough strength to regain his composure. He stood and clearing his throat began his dedication.

"Life has been taken from this temporal body which housed the noblest and gentlest spirit as one ever met on this earthly sphere. My friends, before you lays a woman who aptly fits the description taken from the reading of the Psalm. Noted for her munificence to the poor, Brigid was a dependable acquaintance to many, a steadfast friend to a few and devoted mother and grandmother to kin. Some say she descended from St. Brigid the goddess of poetry and wisdom, daughter of the fire god. As the Lord is my witness and not to offend him in any way, I believe that this might have been the truth. She spoke no malice, was forthright and frank with the facts and always lent a helping hand to those less fortunate than herself. Although she never graced my house or God's house, she shared her own with me on many occasion. We often reminisced about the land and about our ancestors while we enjoyed one of her hearty meals of fish and bruise, baked, stuffed squid or mulligan stew. Embodied in one person was simplicity and complexity; the simplicity of merely offering her guests a meal and the complexity of offering physical and spiritual healing. She welcomed all who graced her doorstep. Blacksmiths and bakers, midwives and mariners, mothers and babies, poets and peasants, she made no exception. Advice was any visitors for the taking. Her charity blanketed over miles, warming thousands. Let us never forget our collective crony as we say our final farewells, knowing that the flame of her spirit will not be put out. Just like the flame of Saint Brigid burns to this day at the entrance to Kildare as a beacon of hope for those who believe. To Brigid Pynn's family we pray that the strength, which was always hers and the light, which constantly twinkled in her eye will be handed over to them as we lay her soul to rest."

Delivering the eulogy was a difficult task because Bridie was not a religious woman, to my knowledge she never set foot in a church. She honoured the Lord in her own way, out in the wide-open spaces. Old Charles Pynn, the widowed brother of our most dearly departed took a coughing fit, providing a little relief from the morose moment, the intensity of mourning that had filled the air and from the unconventional tribute that the Reverend had so sincerely delivered. Under any other circumstances Charlotte and some of the other devout churchgoers would have been aghast at this straying from tradition, this unorthodox exequies. Up in the rafters, a pair of eyes glowed, peering down as the organ energetically pumped out the well-loved Rock of Ages.

The congregation escorted the casket down the aisle and into the graveyard behind the church. The little procession came to a halt by a mound of freshly shovelled earth and formed a circle around the gaping hole. With a few more prayers, the ritual was almost concluded. Slowly, slowly, Tommy Three, Charles, Augustus, Will Garland and two other black suited gentlemen began to lower our beloved Bridie into her tomb. From somewhere could be heard a strange low- pitched melody.

"Lady of the hearth, bless the work of your hands."

Breaking into an unrestrained wail.

"Lady of the fire, bless the work of your heart."

Gradually erupting into a full forced, uncontrollable passionate scream.

"*Goddess of the flames keep and guard you, and may Brigid smile down on you.*"

The penetrating, ear-piercing noise was coming from me, bursting forth out of my mouth. Aunt Charlotte grabbed my shoulders and furiously shook me.

"Anne stop it, stop it."

She slapped me across the face; the shocking sting momentarily subdued my strange mystifying behaviour.

"Whatever is the matter with you, whatever instigated this little drama, this disgraceful performance put an end to it immediately. I say but an end to this distasteful outburst now."

But the devil himself had taken hold of my actions. I needed to have that shawl in my possession. I leapt forward out of the group, breaking the human ring, the chain surrounding the grave. The heads bowed in deference to the dearly cherished deceased, looked up as I grabbed a corner of lace. It came away easily into my grasp but slid down in a heap onto the ground. Kneeling to pick it up I noticed a small flat marker with a tiny lamb etched in the corner.

It read:

Gael Pynn
A spark of light
In the dark of night.
August 1898- September 1898

Here lay the dead child in the song. This much Bridie had given to me.

Throwing myself down against clumps of clay and blackened soil, I wept for all that was lost and all that was found. My tears swallowed up by the soil. It was Augustus who bent down to retrieve the shawl and placed it gently over my back.

Back at the house we extended the customary wake, as a few relatives and neighbours gathered for some last lamentations and a little merry making. Hettie Pike, wearing a frilly, starched pinafore over her black wool suit, brought some tasty treats from the bakery and placed them on fancy silver trays about the front parlour. Admittedly, the sitting room had the best décor in the whole dwelling. A soft yellow settee with flowered cushions and matching footstool was the focal point of the salon along with Charlotte's pride and joy, her piano. In the opposite corner from me was a small writing desk equipped with plume and ink. Auntie never ceased to inform anyone who would listen of how she scrimped and saved to buy these few pieces of furniture, her most precious possessions. All the teetotallers were settled in that cozy room, busy sipping from our very best porcelain cups. Doc Nosie had put a pinch of laudanum into my drink.

"Calm the gals nerves, it will, it will."

Totally blasé to the entire affair, lingering about in the shadows, watching several tongues wagging as they murmured platitudes of nostalgia regarding Bridie, I pondered the identity of our guests. Settled on the piano bench were surely Delilah and her rich husband Sam all dolled up in the latest fashion. Her hat was an unbelievable creation and I noticed the sisters Phoebe and Prudence gawking at the volumes of black tulle wrapped turban fashion about her auburn ringlets. A huge purple feather shooting up from behind reminded me of a strutting peacock. And bangles, she had a dozen of them clicking together about her wrist as she tapped her brightly painted finger nails against the Steinways patina. She was a colossal contrast to her departed sibling. Sam twirled a top hat on his index finger, his shoes shone more than any other pair in the room. He reminded me of a plump dove in his soft grey jacket and vest. It was his tie that stood out, that drew one's eye to his attention, as it was a perfect match to his wife's plume.

Having found Phoebe and Prudence and extracted them from the crowd, I told them that I would be back to work the next day. Missing a whole week was quite unacceptable and I didn't want to put my job in jeopardy. They had both been so kind throughout the entire ordeal. Glancing about, my eye caught the Reverend Sweetapple (nick named sweetie pie) in deep conversation with

Charlotte, offering his last condolences while rubbing her gloved hand between his two rather large scrawny ones. I muttered to myself.

"Now wouldn't that be an interesting arrangement, sweetie pie and my aunt."

Three other women, wives of the remaining Pynn brothers, were standing by the mantle in sombre dress and puffing on cigarettes, the latest craze to hit the island. I had half a notion to wander over and request a smoke myself. The mixture that the old Doc had concocted definitely did its job. I felt so relaxed and light hearted. I fancied the threesome, a trio of movie starlets fluttering about in sequined gowns, blowing kisses to an exhilarated audience. Instead, they were sheathed in brooding black, gloomily discussing injuries, illness and fatalities. Comedians they were positively not. I heard strains of music coming from our kitchen. Unbeknown to the demur crowd up front, the scullery group at the back were having a party to celebrate the passage of Brigid. Newfie screech was flowing liberally and the Pynn brothers, whom had each brought an instrument, were playing along with some of the other less sordid visitors who seemed to be snorting back the rum at rather an alarming rate. Lyrical tunes tumbled forth from the makeshift band that were boozy enough to believe they were virtuosos, while the real virtuous obliviously continued their prayers just a few feet away.

Henry Pynn was squeezing notes from an old cardine; his brother Joseph plucked the strings of an ugly stick while Charles added the quirky sound of the Jews harp. Tommy Three had picked up the spoons, slapping them against his thigh. Will Garland's fiddle issued a squawky version of Ise the Bye, while Augustus brought forth his interpretation of the words. In my drug induced haze I could hear him singing in a clear, loud voice. There was no huskiness about his speech. I wondered what had happened, but my mind in its muddled, medicated state could not concentrate and it passed over the tiny miracle of Augustus' vanished whisper. I preferred the company of the rollicking pantry crowd to that of the oppressing grievers situated on the other side of the wall. Taking a little pause in the Pynn's renditions of many old favourites, Charles sidled over to where I was sitting on a stool.

"I gave your father his first tin whistle, I did, I did." He declared.

"What a talent that bairn had, right from when he was just a little gaffer he could make music. Us brothers, we didn't condone what Brigid did but that lad was like our own, continually whistling, frolicking, leaping about with the tiny lass what my sister took in. I mean to tell you we didn't approve of that shenanigan either. But Bridie had a mind of her own. High spirited, determined to be a mother, she never asked for assistance, nor monetary aid from us. Not one cent. She raised that nipper up good. Shadrach was smart too, more brains than the rest of us. Must of come from the father. All the lad ever wanted to be was a fisherman for he loved the sea. He had a problem though, cause he couldn't take that girl with 'im and 'e couldna' leave 'er behind. He were the tree and she the branch. When he finally did leave, that limb it weakened and we feared it would split in two. But she clung to you and the notion that her husband would return. Always I been wonderin', where that boy got too?" Charles seemed to have said his peace and as he wandered off to fill up his tankard, Henry took his place.

"Well now missy, I hear ye got yourself a nice little job selling bonnets. That's good because a gal needs employment till she finds herself a man and settles. Too bad your gran never felt that way. She just up and found that dilapidated shack out there by the lake, took up residence, hermit style and raised her two kids. Can't say as I blame her, how she just went about her own business. Cause we men weren't any too helpful and that naughty Delilah, she was pretty caught up in getting gussied up, flaunting herself in front of all the fella's. I'm sorry now for not allowin' Bridie more of my time. Everyone knows she ne'er had a bad word to say about any of us. She didna' spread her problems around either, and those she had plenty of, with Shadrach and Druscilla bein' in love and all. But she accepted that without argument or struggle. I'd a bin right furious, them bein' like brother and sister, takin' to each other like a couple of beasts, no explanation, no remorse. No siree – Brigid stood solid, she said they were na related, they were just like any other male and female and why shouldna' they be in love. I shoulda' listened to 'er way back then, 'cause they were devoted and they had what mosta' us folks long for all our lives. Maybe we was all just plain jealous of what those two 'ad. When Shadrach packed up and left the harbour we was all wonderin' what come over 'im. But he weren't stupid; he musta' had a reason for leavin' but I'll be the devils own if I knew what it t'wer. Hey littler Annie, I hear your huntin' up your Pa, my advice is search the sea ports, that's were I think 'e might be found. Good luck to ya' and may the charm of ya'r gran go with ya'." As Henry walked off to replenish his liquor I felt a certain relief from the weight of the peculiar one sided conversations with my father's uncles, I headed toward the back door for a breath of fresh air, my head a bit spinney and my innards about to erupt. Someone gripped my arm.

"Not so fast there, hinnie."

It was Uncle Joseph. Stripped of his suit jacket he stood before me in his undershirt, his big hairy arms hanging out, covered in tattoos. He'd apparently got these in China on one of his trips there as a seaman. Rumour had it that he'd lopped of a Chinaman's pigtail as a souvenir and brought it home where he kept it in a dresser drawer. His speech slightly slurred, his eyes rather blood shot, I figured he was intoxicated enough to make this an unpleasant encounter. Not true. He put that shaggy protrusion around my shoulders and gave me a huge, bear hug.

"You're a beauty ye are, ye are. Shadrach would have been some proud of you. He wanted a daughter so badly. He told me once that if he had a daughter what lived, he'd never again ask for another thing. Quite queer it was that he just vanished before you was born. Never could figure that out. It's a wonder Druscilla lived as long as she did without him. Of course she had Brigid beside her all the while. How Charlotte came to the rescue- the meddlesome fool-interfering, sticking her nose in were it didna belong, is another peculiar happening. Well my pretty one, its up to ye to solve these mysteries, now isn't it?"

And with that Joseph toddled off, his great hulk of a body heaving from one side to the other.

I wandered outside into the cool night air, plunked myself on the stoop and stared up at the stars. A whole other world blinked down at me, a world of angels and grandmothers.

CHAPTER 5

1907

THE WILL

Fortune's fabric
penned on parchment.
Perplexing papers
disclosing
blessings and bequests
to hidden heirs.

A few weeks following the funeral, Arnold Baxter, the only lawyer in the district paid a visit. Charlotte was in a fluster. Determined to make a good impression, she'd cleaned the house from top to bottom, prepared a notable afternoon tea and insisted on me wearing my best Sunday apparel. It was a rare occasion that she fussed about her appearance. She'd even gone so far as to put a dab of rouge on her cheeks and to spread her bow shaped lips with some red gloss. I wasn't so sure all this commotion didn't have something to do with the fact that the solicitor was a bachelor and a regular churchgoer. When Baxter had sent a note around announcing his intentions and advising that he had in his possession a copy of Brigid's will, Charlotte was dumbfounded. "A will, that old woman had a will, I don't believe it. I don't, I don't." In anticipation of what the document might divulge, she had quickly contacted the brothers. They were just as astonished at this startling piece of news as Charlotte. Of course, they admitted that there was the property and house that would have to be disposed of, but other than that, "A will? Leave it to our sister to get all serious and legal over a simple matter."

Well I thought, —perhaps it wasn't that simple.

Baxter was a peculiar looking man. He had a big, pock marked, bulbous nose on top of which perched a pair of wire pince-nez. When he talked, his whole face jiggled and the eyeglasses slipped forward so that he was constantly pushing them up with a fat, stained yellow forefinger that had a bad crook in it. As he spoke, his chest heaved expelling air with a little wheeze just like the fireplace billows on a cold morning. I found it difficult to concentrate on what he was saying because I wanted to lean forward and flick the flakes of dandruff off the collar of his black jacket. Aunt Charlotte gave me her 'smarten up' stare as she elbowed me in the rib cage. Bringing out her best manners, she poured a steaming cup of perfectly brewed tea into one of her dainty, china cups. She added a perfectly levelled teaspoon of sugar, a few drops of rich cream and passed it to the lawyer. Baxter dumped a portion into his saucer and proceeded to lap it up like a cat. I knew Auntie would be wishing she had omitted the make up and the Sunday frock, after this display of absolutely outlandish behaviour. I could just hear her saying, "Coming from a professional, no less." She was making me edgy, wringing her hands and bouncing her one knee up and down, a habit she adopted when she was stricken with a case of the nerves. The two of us sat in the parlour opposite Baxter and stared down at the sheaf of papers displayed on the table. It was obviously time to get down to the business at hand.

"To begin with" he gasped, every breath an enormous effort, "I will read the will, then there is the matter of the three letters, one addressed to Miss Anne, one to Miss Charlotte and the third to Shadrach Pynn. Your grandmother, Miss Anne, came to me shortly after your mother was taken ill and seven years after her son had departed Harbour Grace for places unknown. She was of sound mind when the will was prepared and you both must understand that it is a legal document that cannot be tampered with, nor can it be disputed."

Charlotte sniffed and straightened her spine indicating she would never have any intentions of contesting or challenging Brigid's last wishes. I wondered what could possibly be so controversial on the pages arranged before us that might instigate contention. Was there some secret, some hidden hushed-up scandal about to be disclosed, something Bridie had not trusted anyone enough to recount? Baxter began to read.

The Will of Brigid Pynn

September 16, 1907

I, Brigid Pynn, of Harbour Grace in Conception Bay in the Island of Newfoundland, being in perfect soundness of mind do make and ordain this my last Will & Testament.

To Charlotte Soper of this same community, conscientious Aunt to my granddaughter Anne Pynn, I leave and bequeath the eastern parcel of land; one third of my plantation as prepared by the surveyors Blake & Whelan. This property is for her explicit purpose and may be developed, divided or sold at her discretion.

To Oisin Sweetapple, Parson of the Methodist Church in Harbour Grace in Conception Bay in the Island of Newfoundland, formerly of New Orleans Louisiana, my dearest friend and confidante, I leave and bequeath the western parcel of land; one third of my plantation as prepared by the surveyors Blake & Whelan. This acreage is to be utilized for the construction of facilities that will continue to serve the less fortunate inhabitants of the community.

To Anne Pynn of this same community, my beloved granddaughter, I leave and bequeath the central portion of land bordered on the South by Lady Lake, one third of my plantation as prepared by the surveyors Blake & Whelan. Into her keeping I endow all dwellings and outbuildings on this land including my private house and its entire contents. To her, I leave all of my personal effects and the residue of my estate.

To Shadrach Pynn, my only and adored son who has been reported missing seven years, I leave and bequeath my hat pin, now in the possession of his wife Druscilla. It is my vehement desire that my son be found and the pin delivered into his hand accordingly. The pin was a gift to me on the occasion of his birth. The 14-karat gold, eleven-inch stem supports a diamond cluster in a floral shape with an amethyst stone at its centre.

In the event that Shadrach predeceases me, ownership shall revert to Anne Pynn his only living daughter and my granddaughter.

I looked at my Aunt. The blood had drained from her face, which had become chalk white. She clapped her hand over her mouth in an expression of utter astonishment or maybe alarm. I really could not decipher which. I pressed my fingers into the fleshy skin of her arm, encouraging her to say something, but she just looked at me with eyes bulging. Her usual prudish demeanour had vanquished. She was obviously stunned. For myself, I was not shocked or surprised at the contents of the will. I knew that Bridie would have kept her affairs in order and I had surmised, even half expected, with the exception of Sweetapple, whom her chosen beneficiaries would be. What I didn't have any knowledge about however was the hat pin.

Baxter who was hunched studiously over the papers, straightened, panting out that this indeed was Brigid's last will and testament, signed and sealed in his presence. He asked if either of us had any enquiries and if we understood the terms and conditions. Then, spreading the surveyor's charts in full view on the table, he used the nib of his pen, wetting it with the tip of his tongue, to point out the boundaries of each parcel of land. I could see as he spoke the blue ink forming a boundary around the inside edge of his otherwise pink lips. I couldn't stop staring as the ink formed a globule in the corner of his mouth. He explained that the eastern and western rooms were in fact slightly smaller than the main section. Before the ink had a chance to dry, he gathered up the papers, claiming that everything was in perfect order.

"Ladies, I give to you now the letters which Brigid entrusted into my care for the past few years. Anne, here is yours and that of your father's, and Charlotte this is yours. I must retire now into town to deliver to the Reverend Sweetapple the news of his good fortune. If either of you require any further assistance, I beg of you to contact me at my offices at your convenience."

Snapping shut his portmanteau; breathing heavily he hoisted himself out of the depths of Charlotte's favourite armchair. As the chair was relieved of his weight, the squeezed springs popped up, releasing a sound similar to that of wind being emitted from the behind. I had all I could do not to burst into a fit of the giggles. If Charlotte hadn't been so shaken by the terms of the will, I'm sure she too would have found the rude noise quite humorous. Leaning heavily on his cane, Baxter departed down the walkway.

Charlotte opened her mouth as if to speak but choked on the words. She appeared traumatized. I ran to get her a glass of water and patted her on the back until she had recovered from this unexpected constriction of her throat. She handed me her letter and begged that I read it to her. I was not sure that I really wished to do this, as it might have meant that she would expect that I read my letters to her. But she was distraught and for the moment I pitied her and could not deny her request. Over on her writing table was an ivory handled letter opener, which I retrieved from the desktop. With an ominous feeling in my heart and rather a shaky hand, I slipped the sharp edge into the sealed envelope.

Dear Charlotte:

Our lives have always been separated by different beliefs. We are similar to a piece of woven cloth. My values are the weft running horizontal with the land; your viewpoints are the vertical warp, pointing from earth to heaven. The only common thread in the patch of material, which held the cloth together, was our love for Anne. The saddest occasion of my life was the day you took her home to live with you. My son had been out of my existence for seven long years, my beautiful Druscilla lay inert in her coffin and you removed their love child, carrying her away and causing a huge rent in the fabric of our relationship. I had difficulty being reconciled to your actions and understanding that custody would be yours. But time is a great healer. Our darling girl has grown into a healthy young lady. You have my utmost gratitude for all that you have done for her and my blessings for the future. If I could turn back the clock, I would have mended the tear the instant it happened, the very second that it occurred. But, unfortunately our lives are full of mistakes. In the end we can only hope that the good deeds out way the errors. I hope that you will see it in your heart to forgive my personal affronts to you. May the land which now belongs to you, support and sustain you for the remainder of your life. With deep affection,

Brigid.

My Aunt was not a demonstrative person when it came to her innermost feelings. Oh yes, she could display her anger, but anything else; sadness, joy or passion, she always managed to keep hidden beneath her thick skin. Upon hearing the letter, her impervious exterior melted away exposing an uncommon vulnerability. Visibly shaken, she beseeched that I assist her to her bed.

"I require some rest my dearest Anne, I feel quite weak and fear that I may have caught a chill. Please secure the letter in the top drawer of my bureau. You do understand that it is the beginnings of a head cold or influenza causing me to be indisposed and not in the slightest way Brigid's message which disrupts my behaviour."

She almost pleaded with me to be of this opinion but I was not convinced that this was a truthful explanation. Frankly, I did not understand Charlotte's reaction to the will or the letter. To me, both revealed good news.

After settling her down in her room, drawing the curtains and covering her with a feathered eiderdown. I returned on tiptoe to the parlour with an unexpected eagerness to ascertain the contents of my own letter.

Dearest Annie:

To you I have passed the light and I hope the inspiration to continue my work. Move quickly now and take possession of the house. Move expediently to minister to my patients, my friends who will continue to come to Pynn Place with their afflictions. My books, my nostrum notes are in my medicine cabinet. There are purges and purifiers for numerous plights, preparation hints and dosage suggestions are all recorded. But you must use your instinct. I have left a reserve of palliatives but remember to replace your supplies so that they never become depleted. There are cobweb applica-

tions to stop bleeding; there is burnt cream and the white of egg for infected sores. Mouldy bread, powdered dust of seashells and goose grease all make successful poultices. For digestive or stomach ailments, try some of my ground juniper, dogberry extract or alder buds. Coughs have been abated with extract of wild cherry, or for more serious congestion of the chest, spirits of turpentine or kerosene mixed with molasses might be beneficial. Spread an equal mixture of soap, flour and molasses on muslin and apply to boils. This will expunge pus from the festered area. Do not forget that bottled May snow relieves sore eyes and that burnt ash of tobacco works well for incretions. Ingrown toenails are a common complaint of fishermen whose boots are too small and constantly abrade their feet. A drop of hot tallow from a lighted candle will soften the nail and make it easier to remove. The aches and pains of joints can be soothed by applying bottled, brown jellyfish to the throbbing parts; or if this is not successful, try an amulet of dried haddock fin. I mention some of these more recent curatives, as I have not had the opportunity of late to catalogue them.

Even though I leave you for another place, my spirit will remain in Pynn Place with the blessing of St. Brigid upon you.

May Brigid bless the house wherein you dwell

Bless every fireside, every wall and door

Bless every heart that beats beneath its roof

Bless every hand that toils to bring it joy

Bless every foot that walks its portals through

May Brigid bless the house that shelters you.

With my deepest love and affection: Bridie

I folded the letter back exactly on its creases.
Move to Pynn Place?
Take up Brigid's mission?
Pursue the disappearance of my father?

These were three, enormous tasks that Bridie had mapped out before me.

And Charlotte, one must not forget Charlotte. What would she think? I could not imagine. She would brood, opinionate, say that these were unreasonable demands to be placed on a woman as young as I. But I vowed to do what Bridie had asked of me and silently pledged that Charlotte would not stop me.

The third letter should be read. I hesitated for it must be personal. Confidential words, between mother and son were never meant to be read by other eyes. Never meant to be probed by other minds. Never meant to be scrutinized by outsiders or strangers. But, I was neither of these. I was the daughter and the granddaughter. I felt a force within me: a power, primed, eager to pounce, to explode. A sudden spark, a blaze of flame, a warning before my eyes, reminded me of the wolf, looming and formidable. The wolf that had roamed the Island for thousands of years, invading and raiding, thrusting itself onto claimed territory, stopped me. Is that what I was about to do – pillage my grandmother's private property?

I put the letter down.

Another flash, an outburst of white light recalled to my mind the serenity of the swan and its legendary ability to chose its heroes in the battle of life.

I picked the letter up.

A blinding blue radiance reflected off the letter's surface and seeped up my arm. Another arm from another space and another time assisted mine in breaking the seal—and I began to read.

My Son:

I know that we talked on many occasion of the family land in Massachusetts; chattels that our ancestors held title to. You told me many times that you wanted to sail to Boston, to locate and claim the property. You felt if you found these holdings it would be your stake in the future for your wife and offspring. I believe that is why you went away, to seek your fortune. Your departure was abrupt, without warning and we were quite disconcerted. I know that you were grieving and could not be consoled over the death of your wee baby girl. First the shock of her deformities and then her tenuous grip on life just slipped away. You vanished without the knowledge that your beautiful Druscilla gave birth to a second daughter, perfect in every way. In the beginning, a few short letters were the only communication we had and then all contact, all correspondence stopped. Everyone makes mistakes in this life and I admit that I am no exception. I should have given you my hat pin those many years ago. It was your inheritance and would have provided you with prosperity and promise for the future. I leave it to you now in hopes that it will find its way to you and bring you home to the harbour.

With sincerity:

Your proud and loving Mother.

So—it is quite probable that my father sailed to Boston in search of land.

An idea began to form in the recesses of my mind—an idea so infinitesimal, it whispered so softly, that it could be barely heard by my very own ears. An auspicious idea that would take some planning, or rather conniving on my part, in order for it to come to fruition. I knew I could not speak of it, not a mention to anyone, or it would never materialize. Everyone I was acquainted with would construct barriers to prevent its occurrence. For the time being I knew I must hold the secret plan tight within my chest, like a fist clenched about a surprise.

"Anne, Anne – do you hear me?"

It was Charlotte calling.

"I am feeling a little stronger now," she exclaimed.

"I think perhaps my little episode was only a touch of the vapours. Could you be kind enough to bring some tea and a bit of bannock?"

Boiling the kettle, I thought upon Brigid's restoratives and the new life that awaited me at Pynn Place. I figured this was as good a time as any to try my hand at healing. A hot drink of dried brewed hawthorn berries should help my aunt's distress. When I carried it in to her, she was appreciative but she looked so frail lying there upon the counterpane. Forever fastidious, it was strange to see her hair dishevelled, her clothes rumpled and such a worried look about her face. She sat up to sip her tea, as I glanced about her room where absolutely everything had its place. She had always been the most irritatingly meticulous housekeeper. When I was younger she complained continually about fingerprints on the glass and smudges on the furniture. All surfaces had to be dust free and all floors polished. She complained too about my untidy appearance, especially my hair, which she claimed was all mops and brooms. I'm convinced she derived a certain pleasure and satisfaction from the ritual of brushing. She would go at my tresses with a vengeance; yanking a fistful of strands with such strength that I was sure they would rip straight out from the roots. Venting feelings that were pent up inside, the brush would come down with a thud on my scalp and she would tear the bristles through the tangles, tugging and pulling until she was satisfied that order had been returned to my head. I glimpsed quickly at that same hairbrush beside the matching comb and mirror, arranged with precision on her vanity next to her other various toiletries. I had this crazy urge to pick up the brush and address Charlotte's disordered locks; to pay her back for all those painful episodes I had endured. Her hair was an unimportant aspect of her looks. Thin, brown and straight, it hung limply about her wrinkled face. In her youth she kept it short but lately she tied it back in a knot at the nape of her neck, giving her an even more austere look. If asked, I could not say what her most attractive feature was. She was plain and grim. The yearning to attack her scull vanished when she asked,

"And your letters Anne, what did your Grandmother inscribe?"

She laughed her little nervous laugh.

"Did she divulge her best kept secrets? I jest of course."

I was careful how I answered her.

"Auntie, she only elaborated on the house, which is to be mine. She trusts that I will continue to provide willing, caring hands to serve the abandoned, destitute and feeble sufferers in the town. As she mentioned in her will, it is her earnest plea that her pin find its way to my father."

My little remedy seemed to be having an effect and none to soon either; as Charlotte's eyes were fluttering.

"You must sleep now Auntie and when you awake I am sure you will be feeling much better."

My aunt slept on her bed, in her house with whatever demons possessed her and with whatever angels the good Lord saw fit to guard over her. My grandmother slept in her coffin, beneath native soil delivered of her restless spirits. She did not pass easily from one world into the next. With her departure she had unburdened herself and enlightened me. It was clear to me that the ever-searching wolf would have to unearth answers to questions for the swan to be at peace.

CHAPTER 6

1919

THE HAT PIN

Pin or Pynn,
Trinket or trophy?
Do not trifle
nor tamper
with the jewels.
The talismans
of time.

My life had never been so complicated. There were so many roads down which to travel. Without delay I realized that I needed to continue my work at the millinery so that I could save up enough money to put my secret plan into action. Also, I was obligated to honour Bridie's wishes and relocate to Pynn Place as quickly as possible. But before I did that, I was compelled to find my father and present him with his fortune. Surely that was what it was; a treasure of exquisite gems captivatingly arranged in the form of a hat pin. Were the jewels authentic? Bridie obviously believed they were. On the day that Baxter presented Charlotte and I with the will and Auntie feigned her indisposition, I searched my mother's box and found the pin. I decided then and there to take it to the sisters for advice. Someone in the village had told me on a previous occasion, that Prudence and Phoebe had acquired a certain amount of expertise with gemstones from their father. Perhaps I contemplated, with a little bit of luck, they might be able to determine the pin's origins and verify if it was bona fide, maybe even locate someone to estimate its value. Until I was able to clear up these matters I would be unable to transfer my belongings and myself to Pynn Place and therefore, I would have to find a tenant for Bridie's house. It would not be safe or appropriate to leave it empty and unattended while I continued with the pressing business at hand. I considered placing an advertisement in the Harbour Grace Standard. Someone might respond who was interested in leasing the house for a short term. I reckoned that Oisin Sweetapple might have some suggestions, since he was now the owner of the adjacent property. I knew that he lived alone in the clerics rooms behind the church but through his connections with the parish, he might be acquainted with someone who was looking for accommodation. For that reason I made a mental note to pay him a visit and also to inquire about his proposals regarding his share of the property.

On my next working day, the sisters were already at the shop when I arrived. They had busily begun the decorating of the glass showcases in preparation for Christmas. The holidays were just around the corner, only a few weeks away. They were creeping up on us very quickly and we had to make the most of every opportunity, every spare moment so as to be ready for the anticipated increase in business. Extra special items, which had arrived by ship from Europe and the Americas into St. Johns had been delivered by train to Harbour Grace and brought to the shop to be sold for the festive occasion. Some of the articles were quite extravagant and I personally doubted if they would be purchased. I wondered if there was anyone rich enough to afford them. Certainly they were out of the reach of the likes of Charlotte and I. There were however, some very pretty, less expensive trinkets, which I was sure would lure those folk with fewer coins in their pockets onto the premises. I even brought Bridie's beautiful chair cushions along to use as props in the display. The cheery, crimson material was perfect for the season and the glitter of the gold braid blended well with the sparkle of the jewellery. The three of us worked together pinning brooches, hanging pendants, necklaces and bracelets over the puffy contours of the pillows. As a finishing touch, I cut some snowflakes out of white paper and tossed them randomly about in the showcase. We took a step back, admiring our handiwork very pleased with the exhibit, which we had created.

"Prudence, Phoebe, I have a hat pin which belonged to Bridie and I wondered if you would be so kind as to take a look at it? If you would be able to tell how old it is, to give me some idea of its value and perhaps suggest where it might have come from?"

On impulse, I just blurted out what had been going on in my head. I could tell by the expressions on their faces that the sisters were excited to participate in the little evaluation. They were both quite knowledgeable when it came to gold, silver and precious gems.

Their father, Edward Brown had been a watchmaker and goldsmith in England; a shrewd businessman, he passed his astuteness and experience on to his girls. The story went that when the sisters flowered, bloomed into young womanhood, their wealthy and recently widowed patriarch decided to seek even more prosperity in America. He journeyed across the Atlantic with his family and very valuable cargo; trunk loads of merchandise beneath in the hold. The unfortunate group met with disaster just off Newfoundland's coast when pirates took possession of their ship and seized its costly contents. The father trying to defend his family and his riches was shot. The ship too was left maimed and floundered several days in high seas until some fishermen from Harbour Grace happened on the looted vessel and came to the rescue. The girls were transported ashore and remained there ever since. Luckily for them, some of their assets had been packed onto a boat, which had sailed at a later date and they were able to recover those belongings and start up their own little shop.

Prudence smoothed the soft edges of a chamois down on the counter surface and I positioned the hat pin on top, in full view of the two scrutinizing pairs of eyes. Each of the women had their own loupe attached to a chatelaine about their waists. Almost in unison, they brought it up to their eyes and peered at the pin looking for blemishes or imperfections.

"Flawless in my opinion," stated Phoebe.

"Indeed, indeed,' Prudence reiterated. "As to its value, I can't truthfully say, since we have been out of the market for quite some time. But, it is worth far more than you imagine, I can assure you of that."

Phoebe held it aloft and the diamonds sparkled.

"Anne my dear, with your permission, we will present it to a gentleman, an artisan who comes but once a year in the spring to our little town and he will be able to appraise the piece and give an account of its history. I am sorry that you will have to wait such a long time, but be patient and in a few months when our friend arrives, your answers will be forthcoming."

I put the pin back in its case and thanked the two women profusely. For the rest of the afternoon, the three of us finished decorating and continued to wait on customers.

On the way home I dropped my advertisement off at the newspaper offices and decided to pay a call on the Reverend as the priory was just around the corner from the Standard's building. The Harbour Grace Methodist Church had undergone its fair share of grief. It was completely destroyed by fire in 1850. The building erected in its place a year later burned to the ground in 1904; the edifice built to replace the second desecrated structure stood strong and firm. It had had many clergymen over the years including Oisin Sweetapple's father, Finn. Apparently, the Senior Sweetapple read the bible to his only son every day from his birth, preparing him eventually to take the cloth. He was not disappointed. Oisin left Harbour Grace at the tender and vulnerable age of eighteen for Massachusetts, to delve into his religious studies. Four years later he was ordained a minister. He had several posts in the United States, including his last one in New Orleans. Over the duration of his ministerial service, there was always an annual visit home; allowing a sojourn with his parents and a re-acquaintance with his birthplace. After forty years of preaching, the parson had returned to his beginnings and to the church in which he was raised and where he had obtained his roots.

Standing in the front walk, I looked at the white- framed building before me, its spire ascending up into the heavens. If ever a building could give a person spiritual inspiration, it would be this one. Proceeding around the back where the living quarters were located, I raised the brass angel door- knocker, letting it clank several times. Half expecting to be greeted by Sweetie Pie, I was quite taken aback when a rather attractive young man whose hair was as white as snow opened the door.

"Come in, come in."

My hesitation encouraged his genuine friendliness.

"Now, who might you be?" he asked, as he ushered me in by the elbow.

Admittedly I was embarrassed. A pink blush suffused my face; probably making my freckles stand out in alarm.

I sheepishly murmured, "Anne Pynn."

I was rather perplexed, as the young man had not removed his hand from my arm.

"That would be, THE Anne Pynn, granddaughter of Brigid, would it not?"

Still discomfited by the touch of his skin against mine, I merely nodded

"Well now, Anne Pynn, what can we be doing for you?"

I tried to get a grip on the strange sensation that had spread itself throughout my body. A stirring that speeded up my heartbeat and intensified my breathing.

"Perhaps you might introduce yourself to me." I suggested, taking a step away from him.

"Ah yes, you wouldn't be knowing, would you? I am Oisin's grandson, Finn Sweetapple, all the way from New Orleans. I'm visiting my grandfather for a few months. I come every year to help with chores and it seems this year to help with his plans for his newly acquired property. Today he is out visiting some of his parishioners but he should be returning soon. Is it, that you wish to speak with him?"

Trying to be all professional and proper, I told him that I had some business concerns to discuss with the reverend.

"Sit ye down and we'll have some tea and a chat while we wait. It's not often that I get to talk with such a pretty lass."

Could there be any harm in an afternoon fete with such a good-looking male specimen, I asked myself. What would we converse about, I wondered?

As we talked, I learned that Finn Sweetapple, all the way from New Orleans, was a good ten years older than myself. I learned that he had a very scientific brain being a doctor of medicine. Irish parents, who strongly favoured education, had raised him. What fascinated me the most was his passion for Celtic myth and his ability, indeed his desire to connect his own family history with that of the fabled Fenians.

"I love to talk," said Finn. "Do you know anything about the Irish folk hero Fionn MacCumhail?" he asked.

I shook my head.

"Well, my great grandfather was named Finn after the legendary champion. Fin cumhal means white cap and my great grandpa had masses of white hair when he was born, just like mine. According to myth, when the fabled towhead Fionn MacCumhail was born, he was thrown out of a castle window into the moat by orders from his own grandfather, who feared that the boy would someday take over his kingdom. It was expected that the babe would drown but miraculously, he swam to the surface holding a large fish in his hand. This was the salmon of knowledge from which he ate and became very perceptive and very intelligent. He was able to solve whatever problems came his way. He also became an athlete, an amazing runner. His followers were known as the Fenians. He had a son called Oisin and a grandson named Oscar. My great grandpa, Sweetapple was also a very clever man, some say even a genius. He became a crusader and his followers were the people of God. His son, my grandfather Oisin, inherited the white hair but not the mind. He was not of scholarly persuasions, not an academic. But he was a thinker, a dreamer and a romantic. He can compose the most beautiful verse. Did you know he was a poet?"

I shook my head.

"Am I boring you with my tale?" he asked.

"Not at all, not at all." I replied. "Please finish the story."

I was entranced by the folklore and the musical lilt of Finn's voice.

"Well, to be the son of Finn Sweetapple was not for the faint of heart, nor the sentimentalist. He wanted offspring that were brilliant, bold and robust, who would follow in his footsteps spreading the Gospel. He sent his son to the best school to prepare for his predetermined future. He insisted upon his son finding a mate in order to propagate the family name. Oisin survived, but only just. He graduated as a minister and married a woman he did not love.

They had one son – my father – whom they named Oscar. To the contrary, the fictional Oisin MacCumail fell in love with a princess named Niamh who it is said had a pig's head. When the couple married the swine's snout and indeed all it's ugly features disappeared, replaced with a ravishing beauty."

Somewhere in the corridors of my mind there was a familiarity about the narrative, I wondered, had I not heard the anecdote before?

Finn continued, "Oisin and Niamh left the place of his birth and journeyed far away, he was gone for three hundred years. Do you think my grandfather will live 300 years?"

"You joke of course, for t'would be a miracle."

"Oisin Sweetapple was not a happy man but at least he fulfilled the commands of his father, honouring his wishes and making him a proud and blessed man. Oisin loved the land of his birth and returned whenever opportunity presented itself. It was here that he wrote some of his finest ballads and outstanding odes."

"Yes," I interjected, "and now the Reverend has been here in Harbour Grace for several years, fortunate to have been posted to his favourite niche and fortunate too for his parishioners, as we all love him so dearly."

"Ah but, Finn Sweetapple would have said that it was divine intervention, providence that returned his son to his origins. Sometimes I wonder if the family Sweetapple tried to fashion their lives after the MacCumhails or if it was just chance that there were so many similarities. Sometimes I am certain that there is a spiritual connection.

"What about your father Oscar? Did he ever come here to Newfoundland?"

"No, he never did, nor did he inherit any of the family characteristics or devotional tendencies. He was a shrewd businessman. He had many medical problems and died of a heart attack at the young age of thirty-five. The one strange thing about my father was that he married a woman who became my mother, named Aideen. Now wouldn't you just know that Oscar, the son of Fionn MacCumhail also had a wife with the same name! Doesn't life deal out the most bizarre coincidences."

"And what about you Finn with the white hair, are you liken to your ancestors?"

"Oh yes, I am quick witted all right, a dapper gigolo don't you think?"

"I believe you have quite a jocular disposition and a gift of the gab, if you pardon my saying so."

"I'll pardon anything you say, I like to hear you talk, to listen to the rhythm of your voice. What about the background of the ravishing red haired maiden standing here before me? My grandfather told me if it weren't for your Aunt you would be an orphan, your mother being deceased and your father having disappeared. I rather wish you were an orphan then I could take you in."

The Reverend returning from his pastoral visits arrived just in time to save me from what I feared was shaping up to be an awkward situation. At first he looked slightly perplexed to see his grandson sitting quite close to me, the granddaughter of his departed neighbour. But almost immediately he grinned and welcomed me with a shake of his hand.

"How can I be of assistance to Miss Pynn on this busy wintry afternoon?" he asked with extreme politeness. Right at that moment I decided to tell him the truth about my undivulged plan and also my dilemma about the empty Pynn Place.

"I do not wish to waste your valuable time, kind sir, so I will get directly to the point. As you are most probably aware, I am now the owner of Pynn Place. My grandmother intended for me to move in as soon as possible. For quite personal reasons I am contemplating a voyage to Boston, most likely in the spring and until I return from my trip I will continue to live with my Aunt. In strict confidence I tell you I am hoping to find my father in Boston for I have it on good authority that he may be there. So it is my intention to rent out Pynn Place until my homecoming. I am wondering if you know of anyone who would be interested in letting the house and land for that period of time?"

A look passed between grandfather and grandson. I worried that I had overstepped the mark of good manners.

"Oh dear, I don't think I have explained my circumstances very well." I said, glancing at the two men and then with downcast eyes, heaving a sigh of frustration.

"Now Anne Pynn, you have described your plight quite satisfactorily and I am about to offer to you a solution." Remarked the elder of the two gentlemen.

"How would it be if Finn here moved in? Our living quarters at the manse are cramped and we both need a degree of privacy. If he were living at Pynn Place, he could continue to assist me and at the same time take on the maintenance tasks at your grandmother's."

I found I was staring at the two men, not quite knowing how to respond. A sense of relief that my problem could be so easily resolved washed over me but I also felt my heart fluttering, a warning to be careful.

"Well, Anne Pynn, are you going to deny me the opportunity to come to the aid of the damsel in distress?" Finn pressed, beaming at his grandfather's suggestion.

In a split second I made a decision.

"Yes, I think that arrangement will be quite satisfactory for both of us. You may move in at your convenience. Hopefully it won't take too long to relocate your belongings and settle at the old premises. Now, I really must be going, my Aunt will be worrying, as she always does, about my whereabouts."

Finn, who had been sitting on an ottoman during this entire exchange stood upright and before I was able to retreat, grasped my hand.

"Good day to you then Anne Pynn. I trust I will have the pleasure of your company many times in the not too distant future."

His touch ignited unknown sensations within me, causing unsteadiness on my feet and giddiness about my head. As though a net had been dropped over me, I felt caught and unable to move in any direction. I told myself to breathe in and out, in and out. I knew if I didn't promptly take control of what seemed to be a rush of blood throughout my entire body that I might pass out or crumble and melt into the arms of this strange young man. Finally, I forced my feet to go one in front of the other and I made an escape out into the frosty evening air. Whatever had come over me?

Arriving home, I prepared myself for Charlotte's usual onslaught but luckily for me she was calm. Her chief concern was where I was going to live. I reassured her that for the time being I would continue to reside with her and explained that Finn Sweetapple would be occupying Pynn Place for at least several months. Charlotte's eyebrows rose at the mention of this plan. "I truly think it would have been appropriate if you had discussed this course of action with me, prior to approaching Sweetapple," she declared in a stern voice. "But I am pleased that you intend to stay here with me and not do something silly, like remove yourself to Pynn Place. I know how impulsive you can be and as always, I am concerned for your well-being. Have you made any decisions about the hat pin?" she asked.

Before I could collect my thoughts to give her some kind of answer, without actually lying, she astounded me by saying that she thought that I should sell it.

"It will bring a good price, that pin, it will, it will and God knows that the idea of delivering it into the hands of your father is hopeless."

I wanted to jump down her throat in retaliation but I was not about to release my clandestine intention of travelling to Boston in search of my father. I knew that she would absolutely refuse to let me go. I was determined to plot the voyage without her knowledge. I planned to be safely aboard a steam ship before she discovered my absence. I neither agreed nor disagreed to sell the pin. I did not start an argument as I realized that she was in good humour and I wanted to keep it that way. Using my better judgement, I decided it would be best to change the topic of conversation as quickly as possible.

"We must begin to prepare for the Christmas celebrations. Holidays are only a few weeks away." She cast a pondering glance over the rim of her glasses in my direction. Scrutinizing me, contemplating whether to pursue the issue of the hat pin or to let it pass.

CHAPTER 7

1918

CHRISTMAS

The Creator's gift of faith.
A grandmother's gift of hope.
A young man's gift of love.
Past faith,
future hope.
Discovering
the greatest of three
is love.

A message came by way of the white horses. Thrown up on the shore in a green bottle. I found it on a day that I had let down my defences and agreed to go walking with Finn. He was so persistent, asking me every time we inadvertently crossed paths to accompany him on a winter ramble along the coast. I tried to avoid any exchange of pleasantries, tried to escape his roving eye. I asked him on one chance encounter if he wasn't superstitious about meeting a red haired woman.

"Aren't you worried it will bring you bad luck?" I queried.

He just threw back his head and roared with laughter.

"Not at all, not at all." He was deviously mimicking me. "Oh we are meant to be together, you and I. I have it from good sources. And there is nothing either one of us can do to change it."

I truly tried to discourage a friendship; but he was steadfast.

Finally, the day came when I hadn't the strength to resist his advances, to ward of his attention. Truthfully, I did not want to. I half believed him, this mysterious man who had quite suddenly appeared in my life. Half believed that it was destiny that flung us together. I no longer wanted to neither fend off contact with him nor rebuff his presence. I wanted to see him, talk with him. I wanted him to touch me.

I trembled to think that I was falling in love.

On the day selected for our sojourn, I walked to Pynn Place and from there we set out on a spirited romp across the frosted fields, down the slippery rocky cliff to the beach where ballycaters spread along the waters edge. The air was calm, clear and cold, bringing tears to my eyes as it bit my insides when I inhaled. We held hands and it felt so good, so right. Our wet mittens were frozen together and we couldn't let go. I remember thinking that Charlotte would be mortified.

"Why do you elude me, Anne Pynn?" Finn asked.

I tried to explain to him, the best I could.

"It is my Aunt. She is so possessive of me, ever since my mother died. Having lost her father and sister, the people dearest to her; I think she fears that I too will be taken from her. Her anxiety is not just that I might die but that I might leave her. She is a pious, resolute old maid. I cannot recollect that she has ever had a friendship with any man, let alone fallen in love with anyone. It seems to me she abhors any male, female relationships. She loves me of course, in her own way, but she cannot let me go. I, in turn, do not want to create grief between us. For the moment she is the only family that I have, at least until I find my father."

Finn smiled acknowledging that he understood my predicament.

"Well, I can see that it will be my job to change her attitude. I cannot have you fussing and fretting about your Aunt every time you are with me. I'll undertake to win her over, reduce her worries and convince her that I am not about to steal you away. With her permission, I will have the chance to properly court you. Then on your part, there will be no reason for refusal."

Sauntering slowly along the shore we noticed that a few fishermen had drilled holes in the ice. They sat patiently waiting in their homemade, wooden huts, with the backs to the wind and the fronts open to a burning pile of bavin and brushney. Those small fires warmed their hands and feet, preventing them from becoming scrammied. With the exception of those few diehard blokes, we were alone. I felt the gentle pressure of an arm about my waist. I thought Finn was about to take me in his arms when instead it was he who spied the bottle that had been tossed into a rocky crevice with other riff- raff, which had been expelled, heaved up from the ocean floor. There was a cork in the top and when held up to the light, one could see something inside. Grasping it by the neck, Finn smashed it hard against a boulder and it shattered sending green shards of glass in every direction. A scrunched sheet of stained brown paper fluttered to the ground. Picking it up, I discovered it to be a handwritten note. In some places the weeping ink had run across the page, crying to be read.

"Celebrate, for I will spread above your heads, a mantle bright to guard you." I looked questioningly at Finn.

"These are words, he said "from the Hymn to St. Brigid; I recognize them from the Book of Praise. It is one of my grandfathers favourite songs."

I knew then with certainty that the message came from my grandmother; somehow passing the barriers from one world into another. I told Finn that he might think me peculiar, even a bit unstable but that I believed with all my heart that this was Bridie's way of communicating with me, with both of us.

"I never met your Gran," Finn admitted, "but I have heard about her unusual powers from several of the villagers. Some even speculate that she may have descended from the ancient pagan sea Goddess; a mermaid dressed in the water's blue with pearls about her neck."

I could not believe what he was telling me, what I was hearing. He described exactly the creature in the hallucination of my illness. Suspicious by nature, I asked myself how could this man have this knowledge. Here he was still virtually a stranger to me, telling me personal, private things. Had Brigid with all her powers sent Finn to me? Sceptical about him but at the same time drawn to him, I squeezed his hand.

"Never fear, I do not think that you have lost your senses. I don't doubt that if Brigid wanted to communicate with you, she could. Sometimes I receive messages from my departed ancestors too. It is a phenomenon I cannot explain. These words coughed up from the sea are surely your Gran's way of saying that she will protect you. They are tidings of joy, we are meant to be happy, we are meant to be together. Think about this: Christmas is drawing near. We should make merry, celebrate and honour your grandmother's wishes. For me this will be the best Christmas ever, for I have you to share it with."

Could I trust this man? He was certainly persuasive. I thought about the words, "Celebrate, for I will spread above your heads a mantle bright to guard you." Had Bridie really sent this message, had she in fact sent Finn? Or, had Finn himself concocted this whole scenario in order to reel me in? *A mantle above your heads.* What did that mean? I thought about the caul in its leather pouch safely tied about my neck. Where the two connected: the mantle over our heads and my father's caul? My heart of hearts told me this was true and that Finn and I were somehow linked now that we had shared this note.

"How will we celebrate then?" I asked.

"In as many ways as we can possibly think of. Look Anne, look over there." He pointed to the group of rocks that make up Harbour Grace Islands; Eastern Rock, White Rock, Ragged Rock, Long Harry Rock and Salvage Rock. They looked like the humped backs of grey whales off in the distance but I could see two figures perched on White Rock. "They're puffins, a pair of puffins. Here in Newfoundland we call them clowns of the sea because of their multi-coloured beaks and orange feet. Sshhh! If we listen carefully we might hear their deep, throaty, cooing noises that almost sound like they are saying 'Hey All. Hey All." See, they are swinging their heads from side to side and tapping their bills together, the bonding activity of mates. It is a good omen Finn because as a rule, they do not make an appearance until the spring. They have given me courage; I feel brave enough to take on an army. Lets go back and tell Auntie and Sweetie Pie, oh dear, I mean your grandfather; that they are about to experience the time of their lives. We will host an old fashioned Christmas with all the trimmings, one to truly remember."

On the day of the puffins, as I came to refer to it, Finn and I cut down a balsam fir and dragged it back to the house. Already having approached the Reverend with our inspiration, we found his reaction, as one would anticipate, entirely positive. He cheerfully added some suggestions to the list of activities we had devised and offered to help organize the events. I could tell he was looking forward to the excitement. The tree, which was a perfect specimen, was uniquely formed. It reminded me of a picture I had seen of a ballerina poised in all her splendour. The gauzy material of her verdant dress floating about her, tight at the waist and pyramiding out down to her ankles. The branches splayed from top to bottom, the silvery, green pine needles forming a gossamer gown, pirouetting about the trunk. The tree was a bid to the charitable side of Charlotte's rather lacking generosity, in the hopes of winning her over to accepting our proposal of a grand celebration. As one would expect, she vehemently protested. First, she counselled that Christmas should be a religious affair and that the frivolities that we had in mind in no way honoured the birth of our Lord. But I felt there was a deeper reason for her reluctance. What it was, I could not fathom. After Finn had erected the tree in a pail of sand to keep it upright, he told us that he must be on his way and he pressed my hand, offering what little reassurance he could against Charlotte's adversity. The second he was out the door, she was off on one of her tangents. Becoming increasingly more agitated, she paced about the room spewing some blather about the "boy" being a heathen, a non-believer and that I would be well advised to stay clear of him and his pagan schemes. Her concern seemed centred around my relationship with Finn and not about the upcoming festivities.

"I simply will not tolerate you being together, its unhealthy. He's conspiring to take you away, he is he is," she yelled at me across the room.

"Balderdash, we're only trying to have a bit of fun, to celebrate."

I knew I daren't tell her about the message in the bottle but I did let it slip out that Oisin had already given the festivities his stamp of approval. Incredibly that news quietened her erratic mewling. As though she had the weight of the entire world upon her shoulders, she sighed in agreement. She was so difficult, so unpredictable.

"We have reached an armistice then?" I asked.

"I will not stop you but I do not give you my blessing either."

She replied.

Why was she confusing our partying with a relationship manifesting itself between Finn and I? Why did she distort a simple friendship into meaning a commitment to each other or a betrothal? Maybe she saw our companionship as something she had never had, something she had yearned for all her life. Maybe she was jealous.

Finn returned the following day, all rosy- faced from the cold to decorate the tree. He brought some delightful, glass baubles donated to the cause by his grandfather. There were several of these sparkling ruby red balls that we hung from the branches along with streamers of silver tinsel. I had strung old Christmas cards and some colourful wooden beads on green wool and these too, we draped from the crest to the base. From a basket of fruit, we selected the choicest oranges and apples and placed them in the arms of the thickest boughs. A few days earlier I managed to sneak out, unawares to Auntie, into Henrietta's and purchased some peppermint walking sticks, which I brought out of their brown paper bag. Finn laughed with glee as he popped a piece of one into his mouth and helped me to dangle the remaining ones in some vacant spots amongst the sprigs of evergreen. Then he reached into the pocket of his tweed jacket, extracted a long ribbon of tinkling, jingle bells and a hallowed, silver star.

"They're from Bridie's," he said, "I found them in one of her old cupboards and brought them along. I hope 'tis all right?" His mirth was catching. I grabbed his arm and we swung about in *do si do* fashion. Out of the corner of my eye, I caught Charlotte watching our playful antics. And wondered what she was thinking?

The night before the nativity, our kitchen fairly groaned with delicacies; purity syrup, eggnog, rum soaked fruitcake and jam jams. The whole house was saturated with the aroma of lamb, which was slowly roasting in readiness for the morrow. Turnips, carrots and potatoes, peeled and sliced were soaking in pots of cold water, prepared for boiling. In my enthusiasm, I had invited the Pynn brothers to partake of our Christmas banquet. On Tib's Eve however, only Finn and his Grandfather would dine with us on the traditional sun cured cod in a savoury sauce. To her credit but much to her chagrin, Charlotte had helped prepare the special fish dish. I had selected a little gift for each of the men and for Auntie. After the sun had set I hoped to play the piano so that the four of us could enjoy an evening of carol singing. At the same time we could rehearse some of the tunes, enabling us to entertain our guests on Christmas day. I was not the best musician in the world but I had been practising a few songs for this special occasion. I had forgotten to ask Finn if he played an instrument. If he did, he could accompany me. We could play along together and give a little performance.

Even though Finn and Oisin arrived bearing gifts and good cheer, initially there was tension in the air emanating specifically from Charlotte. She kept her head lowered and concentrated on avoiding eye contact with either of our guests. Sitting down to the meal, Oisin assumed the duty of giving the blessing. It was as though God himself had graced the table for the festivities. Watching Charlotte from behind my folded hands, her lips parted and the slightest smile escaped.

"Amen, amen." We uttered in unison.

The meal passed pleasantly and although Charlotte was in the beginning ill-at-ease, attending to duties in the kitchen in a servant fashion she eventually relaxed. Her nervousness and jitters waned. As we gathered about the fireplace and I began my fleetingly rehearsed program, she softened and joined in the singing. Finn had a strong deep voice. He carried the melody, becoming the soloist and made it easier for the three of us to blend in as the chorus. I thought we sounded pretty accomplished, considering the small amount of practise we had. Finishing all the pieces I was capable of playing, I clapped my hands and everyone tagged along, giving ourselves a well deserved round of applause.

It was time to share our little tokens of friendship. The giving and receiving of these expressions of peace and good will was filled with excitement and drama. I was eager to see the reaction of our guests as they opened their presents chosen with individual consideration and thought. For Oisin, I had fashioned Saint Brigid's cross from a length of hemp. Usually, these crosses woven with wheat or rush were formed to look like the Eye of God, the arms of the cross being all the same length. Hung on a wall, they offered the blessing and protection of the Saint to the owner and his home. The Reverend was delighted. He brought Charlotte and I a Yule log, which we placed at the back of the hearth. It was an old Newfoundland custom to take the ashes from the Christmas log and toss them over the roof. They were said to protect the dwelling from fire during the coming year. Auntie made both Finn and his grandfather very fine monogrammed linen handkerchiefs, which they appreciated exclaiming with gusto, "How appropriate" and "Just perfect."

Opening her parcel from me, Auntie admired the soft mauve beret that I managed to purchase from P & P's. She set it jauntily on her head and went to take a look in the mirror over the fireplace. Smiling, she declared, "It is first-class." Still grinning she handed me a carefully, wrapped package, "I admit a definite deviousness in this particular selection for you dear Anne."

Tearing off the brightly embellished paper I discovered a small gold wristwatch. Surprised—-did not adequately describe my feelings. It was a very splendid gift; my intuition told me that it was Auntie's way of making amends for all the disagreements and confrontations that we had lately experienced. Not wanting the situation to become too sentimental, Charlotte humourlessly suggested that I might now manage to be on time. The moment had arrived that I had been waiting for with considerable anticipation. It had taken me a long time to figure out what to give Finn. I wanted it to be something useful but at the same time, a reminder of that special holiday. Finally deciding upon a miniature water colouring of Harbour Grace I had signed the back, 'your friend'. Finn loved it.

"It is unsurpassed and to think that you painted it yourself, what talent! And now, for you my dear Anne Pynn, here is a little memento from me to you; may it be the start of a menagerie." It was a pigmy glass puffin.

The crowning glory of the evening was looking westward out the window as darkness fell; for peaking their heads from behind the clouds were the merry dancers, the first sign of the northern lights about to welcome Christmas morn. I will never forget how they blinked down approvingly on my first kiss.

Church bells peeled out over the town as Auntie and I walked into the Christmas service the next morning. A skiff of snow covered the roads and cloaked the trees, creating a fairylike landscape. There was serenity about the entire village that gave it a make-believe aura. With all the circumstances occurring in my life at that time, I felt as though I had been uprooted and relocated in the middle of a fictional novel. Felicitations, good wishes and kind words abounded at the church entrance as parishioners assembled to celebrate the birth of Christ. Just as the service was about to proceed, Finn slipped into our pew, seating himself right next to me. I could feel the warmth of his body close to mine and the deliberate pressure of his leg up against my thigh. Charlotte was unaware of the physical connection between the two of us, as she had forgotten to bring her glasses and without them, she was unable to see past her nose. For once I believed that God was on my side. After the customary readings and traditional hymns, the Reverend ascended the pulpit.

"Good tidings and Merry Christmas to each and everyone." He greeted the congregation. "Last night I had the pleasure of being entertained with a truly traditional repast and an enjoyable round of time-honoured carols. It was one of those carols "The Twelve Days of Christmas", which I base my sermon on today. To some people it is just a delightful nonsense rhyme but it was in fact written in England with the serious purpose of being a catechism song. The twelve days actually begin today on December 25th and end on January 6th. The carol was written as a mnemonic device used to assist or improve the memory. Within the song there are hidden references to the basic teachings of the church. As an example, the "true love" in the tune is not really an earthly suitor but is God himself and the "me" is every baptized person, who is part of the believing community. Each of the days represents some aspect of the Christian Faith. The partridge in the pear tree symbolizes Christ himself. The two turtledoves personify Mary and Joseph or the Old and New Testament. The three French hens stand for the gifts of the magi, gold frankincense and myrrh or the three theological virtues, faith hope and charity. The four calling birds pose as the four gospels or four evangelists, Matthew, Mark, Luke and John. The five golden rings depict the first five books of the Old Testament known as the Pentateuch, which give the history of man's fall from grace. The six geese a-laying reflect on the six days of creation or six days of human labour. The seven swans a-swimming are the seven gifts of the Holy Spirit; prophesy, ministry, teaching, exhortation, giving, leading and compassion. The eight beatitudes are in the guise of the eight maids a-milking .To refresh the memories of those of you who might have forgotten they are: Blessed are the poor in spirit, those who mourn, the meek, those who hunger and thirst, the merciful, the pure in heart, the peacemakers and those who are persecuted for righteousness sake. The nine ladies dancing embody the nine fruits of the Holy Spirit, which are love, joy, peace, patience, kindness, generosity, faithfulness, gentleness and self-control. Of course the ten lords a leaping are the ten- commandments. Again, if your memory is hazy, they are simply put: thou shalt have no other gods before me, do not make any idols, do not take God's name in vain, remember the Sabbath, honour your father and mother, do not murder, do not commit adultery, do not steal, do not bear false witness and do not covet. The eleven pipers piping describe the eleven faithful apostles and finally the twelve drummers drumming illustrate the twelve articles of the apostle's creed.

    The historical accuracy of this carol is often questioned. Some historians say it is just a mythical legend, some theologians say that it is only an anecdote or love song. But my dear, dear friends, we must not let this uncertainty prevent us from benefiting from the words and rejoicing in whatever meaning we each as individuals care to believe." At this point Finn gripped my hand so hard that I was afraid he would crush the bones entirely.

Following the end of the homily, Charlotte and I made a quick escape returning home to the business of the kitchen. The finishing touches were attended to and the table prepared, laden down with an abundance of comestibles. Everyone arrived quite ravenous, having saved up their appetites for the party. When the main course had been devoured, Uncle Henry boomed out "And what's for afters?" Sliding his hand under his belt he withdrew his revolver and aiming it towards the ceiling fired the traditional gunshot to announce the arrival of the Christmas pudding. Upon that customary heralding, I ceremoniously presented the steaming carrot and current dessert with hot rum and brown sugar sauce. Bowls were passed with huge dollops of the appetizing concoction and in very short order all of them were emptied. We even licked the serving spoons, savouring the last few drops. All were sufficed.

Finn pushed back his chair and jumped up from the table. "Its time to go mummering!"

"Mummering" we all bellowed out in unison.

"Yes, yes –Anne find us some costumes."

Down in the root cellar was an old crate where Charlotte stored cast off clothing and worn out linens. I dragged up the dusty, must smelling contraption and all hands delved inside, searching amongst the articles for garments with which to disguise their identity. Auntie, surprisingly appeared to enjoy the concept of concealing herself and after cutting two holes for her eyes in an already ruined pillowcase, she pulled it over her head. Henry, Joseph and Charles blackened their faces with bits of charcoal completing the camouflage with quaint moth-eaten wool caps, which they tugged down over their brows and ears. Oisin used an old burlap potato sack to fashion a horse's head. Tying the corners with string to make the ears and devising a snout by pushing a balled sock out the front, he galloped about the room like a young gelding. Pretty energetic for an octogenarian, I thought. Finn decided to be the horse's ass. He attached a length of rope to a threadbare brown blanket for a tail; grabbing hold of his grandfather's waist he spread the cover over himself and began to emulate the animal's whinny. I found a scraggly discarded beekeeper's hood, which someone had once used to protect himself while collecting honey. Encasing my head in that apparatus, it more than adequately masked my face. I snapped up a leather belt and pretending it was a whip, began tapping Finn on the behind. "Off we go all you Jannies." Laughing and singing, we marched down the street, weaving our way between the lampposts that were hung with resplendent lanterns of the season. Arriving at Will Garland's home, we knocked on his door, calling out "Any Mummers Allowed In?" "Enter, enter." He replied. An odd dwarfish man, he always seemed even shorter standing beside his wife, who towered over him by several inches. They had three mischievous little boys who chased each other about, pushing and pulling, in the front vestibule sticking their tongues out at our queerly robed troupe. Offering us each a glass of grog, husband and wife attempted with little success to guess our identity. Encouraging them to join in our parade we moved on to Augustus', again shouting out "Any Mummers Allowed In?" Augustus greeted us, "Welcome, welcome." I remembered that up until the day of the funeral the man had never been able to find his voice but now it boomed out with great clarity. Himself and everyone who knew him considered the phenomenal return of his vocal chords a marvel. I must not forget to discuss this with Finn as I recalled that Augustus had picked up Brigid's shawl and in the back of my mind, I wondered if this had somehow instigated a cure. Providing a glass of blueberry wine to warm our innards, Augustus requested that we sing for him, which we did with considerable delight. Dressing up in a yellow rain slicker and knee high boots, he then accompanied us as we rambled on toward Henrietta Pikes and then to Prudence and Phoebe's. By that time we were quite full of spirits.

It was as Finn had predicted, the best Christmas ever.

CHAPTER 8

1900-1907

THE JOURNALS

Frenzied fingers
fraught
with words
on pristine pages.
Patches of pulsing
life unfailingly
inscribed.

In the New Year, I was very busy at the shop, rearranging the displays, ordering new merchandise and even trying to convince the sisters to tackle an expansion proposal, which included a men's haberdashery. A spacious, walk-in cedar lined closet with built in shelves on both sides would accommodate the new commodities. Just about enough space was left in the aisle for any gentlemen callers to take a glance at some of the exciting articles that I'd requisitioned. Bowlers, busbies, pork pies, caps, stetsons, trilbys and top hats were delivered and stacked in their boxes in the back hall waiting to be unpacked. I found men's head attire far more intriguing than women's. Personally, I preferred to wait on men more than on women, as they were much easier to please. Men always knew exactly what they wanted whereas women inevitably fussed and fumed over the colour or the shape or the adornments. Quite proud of my latest undertaking, I revelled in any praise that slipped my way. The new venture took up so much of my time that I barely had a thought for my dead grandmother, my dead sister or my dead mother. Repressing my inquisitiveness, I didn't allow myself the slightest opportunity to return to the box. Since the unsettling events of the funeral and the reading of the will, I was unconsciously avoiding the next stage of the journey. I was almost afraid to seek whatever details might be pressed between the pages of my mother's journals. Working extra hours to prepare these items that would be placed on sale to the public had offered a welcomed escape from life under Charlotte's roof. These additional chores and the physical labour provided an excuse to spend less waking hours with her; evading her incessant questions about my emotional state and dodging her curious stares. And stare she did, whenever I had been out gallivanting with Finn. A late winter Saturday arrived and with it, a well deserved day of rest.

    Snuggled beneath the warmth of my feather eiderdown, lingering in those last moments between sleep and wakefulness, I caught the sun rising from the window under the eaves of my attic sanctuary. My own private haven, hidden away from prying meddlesome intruders because the door was locked and the key safely, secretly stowed between the double mattresses. Snow was imminent. I could tell by the smell of the air and from the patterns of frost etched on the glass pane. My mother liked the snow. She made a ritual every winter of going out when the first flakes came drifting down from the sky. Arching her neck back and laughing as she opened her mouth to catch a few of the white drops on her tongue, she said she could tell a lot by its taste: bitter if there would be blizzards, sleet and ice or sweet for a sunny arctic wonderland. Weather conditions were a part of Harbour Grace life and my mother was good at foretelling what elements were brewing. When a big snow fell she would march me outside to draw pictures on the white landscape. Often the two of us would lie side by side in the soft flakes and make giant butterflies with our arms. My mother loved to go sleighing. Dressed in a furry beaver overcoat that drooped down past her knees, a massive woolly cap tugged down below her ears with a long scarf wound about her neck and her hands thrust deep into cosy, fuzzy mittens, she would dump me clothed equally as warm into our bob-sled and off we would go across the snow laden hills. Zooming over the knolls and down the slopes, with wet splotches flying up into my face was the most exhilarating feeling. Being enclosed tightly in my mothers embrace was the safest, secure place. Sometimes Uncle Henry would come and take us out in his horse drawn cutter. We would glide across the frozen turf, the bells on the harness ringing out in the clear frosty air. If he tapped the mare's hindquarters with the tip of his whip she would pick up the pace, galloping boisterously, the rugged terrain beneath her hooves tossing us from side to side while curls of vapour belched forth from her nostrils. Returning home to steaming cups of cocoa with a blob of thick fresh cream floating like an iceberg in the middle of the hot liquid, we would gather around a blazing fire chafing our hands, warding of chilblains and warming the spirit. It struck me recalling some of those precious moments of my childhood that it was a good time to begin reading those journals, penned by my mother's succinct hand. Privately, there in my own little quarters, where I breathed in and out, in and out, calming the nervousness that raced through my veins, I untied the string that bound the package together. There were five journals in total, each dated and titled, each written in Druscilla's large, bold script. A short letter addressed to me introduced the journals.

For My Darling Daughter

Anne

I began writing these chronicles after Shadrach, your father left. They are for you, my darling Anne. They are an account of my life and my relationship with your father. A compilation of my thoughts and feelings, my version of our family history, seen from my eyes, collected together for your eyes. I have written everything down for you to keep, to hold close to your heart. You will read these when I am gone. I want to be sure you have my story and not someone else's rendition. It is after all a love story, a beautiful love story that could be twisted to have an ugly ending. So from mother to daughter I pass these journals to you.

Good omens and bad ones have passed me by, as a forewarning that the time of our physical togetherness, our earthly bond would be brief. As mother and infant we matured side by side on the road of life. Shoulder to shoulder we climbed the majestic white birch. At times you encouraged me upward, at times I lifted you higher. A fork on the road of life appeared where the massive trunk split and diverted in two directions. I veered left moving over to prepare for my journey to the other world while you turned right staying in the earthly sphere. The cleft in the strong trunk of the tree diverged and two branches went their separate ways. Do not tremble at that parting for the union of our psyches will continue for eternity. Even though one day soon I shall leave this earth, you will always have a part of me close to your heart in the words set down on these pages.

Attached to the letter was a still life. As so often happened when seized with emotion, my mother had transferred her thoughts into art. Relative to its length, the painting was narrow. A white tree filled the parchment, its branches growing over the edges, spilling off the page. White branches and waxen leaves were highlighted by a dark cloud on the left. Spears of brilliant orange and yoke yellow tinged the russet leaves on the right. Two figures, mother and daughter, climbed the tree. Two small hands clasped around the trunk, two thin hands stretched skyward and two calloused ones reached down. White hair tangled in white branches. Ruby ringlets locked in vermilion leaves.

Temporarily I was lifted from my bed up into the tree. I felt my mother by my side, her sweet breath upon my face. I wished she were really by my side, to offer advice, to guide me. I wished she could tell me what it had been like to love my father. Had she ever told anyone her innermost longings? Were her feelings similar to those I experienced with Finn? What had she hoped for me, what had been her dreams for her only living child?

A whisper, soft as the rustle of leaves, rose from the painting, "Read on Anne, read on."

CHAPTER 9

Journal 1
1880-1890

CHILDHOOD

Imagine
an angels innocence
a butterfly's purity
a bird's freedom.
Fanciful flight
on wondrous wings.
The chance
of childhood.

Until I was ten, I believed that it was probably my fault that my mother died. No one ever explained the circumstances to me but I heard whispers at night when I was supposed to be in bed asleep. And Charlotte my sister, who was fifteen years older, was always pointing her finger at me saying, "Silly did it. She did, she did." What it was I was supposed to have done I couldn't fathom. The truth of it is that I loved Brigid; she's the only mother I ever knew. I told her one time that I was sorry, truly sorry about my own mother and that I had assumed all responsibility, all the blame for her death. She said that guilt is like a terrible boil and if left to fester, it draws one's goodness into a big, ugly thumping head just waiting to erupt.

"No one is to blame Druscilla, your mother died because her time had come, it was nature's plan."

Then she told me to hold out my hand.

"I'm going to lance that carbuncle once and for all."

She took a long sharp darning needle from her sewing basket and pierced the skin of my palm letting out the imaginary foul rotting pus of the invented abscess. A few drops of blood spurted onto a blanket she had in her lap and I began to cry. Enfolding me in her arms, snuggling me up against her soft warm flesh, we nestled together, rocking back and forth; she crooning in her deep guttural voice until the pain had gone away. Covering the cut with a healing poultice she announced that I was cured of condemnation. That scar is still there, a little white ridge, a reminder of my guilt-ridden innocence.

Brigid had strange remedies for many ailments. The villagers thought she was odd; that she performed some kind of black magic. Some even speculated that her antidotes for sickness verged on witchery, that some kind of voodoo or hocus-pocus was involved in her treatments. But still if illness befell, disability, disease, infection, any variety of infirmities, they came to her for mending. The way I saw it, that's exactly what she did, mend. No miracles were performed just plain patching up, repairing, healing. Throughout my childhood, the sick and the starving limped and staggered up to our door for Bridie's help and she never failed them.

From birth until I was almost ten, I dwelt under a protective roof that encouraged, strengthened and supported both Shadrach and me. Bridie was not only our mother but our teacher. Our schooling took place in the garden, in the kitchen, by the lake under blue skies and clouds and under the moon. She referred to our lessons as sessions of survival, nurturing us in an unorthodox fashion. Together we marched down an irregular drung, an enlightening path, paving it with questions, pursuing common, everyday facts and chasing after the unusual, and the exceptional. We taught each other, your father and I. Right from the beginning, it was unexplainable how our two bodies, two inquisitive minds, created an integral process, challenging, challenging from morning 'till night. Just as we watched the seeds that we planted in the garden ripen and mature, so we saw ourselves flourish under the tender hand of our mentor and mother. From the mud and soil of our yard, we harvested potatoes and vegetables to feed our hungry bellies. In the kitchen we learned to cook and bake. Best of all was fishing in the lake. With our little homemade poles dangling over the waters edge, we would sit for hours side by side waiting for the inevitable bite. Whatever the catch, it was plunked into a bucket which we carried home between us as we chanted the tune "fishy, fishy in the brook." Cleaned and scaled, the fish got tossed into a sizzling iron pan and fried up with onions, fat pork and bread for that evening's meal. I have to tell you Annie that life was simple but wonderful all at the same time. There were special occasions, unforgettable experiences, notable moments that must be recounted; I hope you can picture them in your mind's eye.

Bath time was once a week on Saturday. Bridie had to heat up several pots of water on the wood stove and empty them into a big copper tub. Then Shadrach and I would strip down buck-naked and jump in. It was great fun soaping each other up, splashing and squirting the water over the sides as it spilled out onto the floor in little puddles. Dunking our heads under, we would stare at each other through the bubbles and ripples, *making faces, sticking our thumbs in our ears wagging our fingers; then we would burst to the surface to catch some air. We stayed soaking in that big washbasin until our lips were blue with the cold. Shivering, with goose bumps the size of marbles popping out of our flesh, we would climb out to be rubbed dry. Then the chase was on as we bounded about the kitchen in a game of hallik or tag, always falling in a hysterical heap onto the floor. Sometimes Shadrach would shout, "Hoist your sales and run." Then, instead of tag it was hide and seek. We had the best hiding places: inside Bridie's cedar blanket chest, under her big iron bed or behind the birch armoire. Bridie would come searching, "Come out, come out, wherever you are." She would peer into corners and behind doors pretending she hadn't a clue where we were hidden. When the games were finished we helped empty the water, carrying the sloshing buckets outside and dumping the contents in the garden. Bridie claimed the bath water was the reason we had such a prolific harvest. Lacking all modesty, we took our bath together in that copper tub until the day Shadrach left.*

On November 1 1884, Bridie took us into town for the arrival of the first train. For two five year olds it was a thrilling incident. The railway had been under construction for quite some time and the line from St. John's to Harbour Grace was finally completed. Bridie told us that the length of the track was eighty miles, a very long distance and that the cost of the operation was estimated at four million dollars, a very large sum of money. Bridie was proud of the railway, as several of her brothers had worked on the engineering. Many of the men who toiled with pickaxe and shovel were surrounded with misery and heartache. Through the thirteen years, from start to finish, several riots had broken out, instigated by those inhabitants who believed that evil would befall them if the track were laid on their land. During one disturbance the labourers were stoned and their equipment and instruments stolen away. Despite the turmoil and frequent political opposition, completion was reached and the day would go down in the archives of history.

The last spike was to be driven by none other than Prince George himself who had travelled all the way from Britain for the momentous occasion. The previous week had been a bustle of activity as the townsfolk prepared the streets, festooning them with red, white and blue banners. An afternoon programme was planned for speeches and to honour dignitaries and businessmen whose contributions had been exceptional. A temporary stage erected in front of Ridley Hall, always the centre of social, administrative and economic activities, was draped with bunting and pots of chrysanthemums bordered its stone and brick façade. The women's committee from the Church of England had made miniature union jacks and fastened them to wooden doweling so when held aloft they would fly in the breeze. As we approached the town limits, we saw the crowd jauntily waving the flags above their heads while they awaited the arrival of the train. The Dorcas Society, a Presbyterian Woman's group not to be outdone by their Methodist counterparts, had set up a little booth and was selling sugar cookies and syrup. The 'society for improving the condition of the poor' was wandering amongst the bystanders shaking glass jars under their noses in the hopes that they would collect a few pennies towards their cause. The Masonic Order led a small parade down Water Street followed by the Irish Benevolent Society and the Total Abstinence Society, all waving gaily decorated placards welcoming the Prince. Fraught with eagerness, the spirited spectators, most attired in patriotic colours, jostled each other, all trying to position themselves in a spot, which would provide the best view. The youngest daughter of the Justice of the Peace, Sarah Brown, was to present the Prince with a bouquet of flowers. One of the women, who was part of the planning organization and a friend of Bridie's, came rushing up to our little group quite distressed. Apparently Sarah had come down with the croup. She was laid up in her bed and unfortunately would be unable to take part in the ceremonies. His Royal Highness must be revered with the nosegay of posies from a young child. The woman was in search of a substitute for Sarah and as soon as she caught sight of me scrunched close between Bridie and Shadrach she announced that I was the perfect stature. Size was of the utmost importance, as a white fur coat and hood had been made for Sarah to wear. Insisting that I try on the rabbit skins and at the same time encouraging me to practise a proper curtsey, the woman was satisfied that she had found the ideal replacement. She hustled off to perform some other perfunctory duties deemed necessary in preparation for the regal greetings. My hand in Bridie's became sticky with sweat and little ripples of nerves chased about in my stomach. Having never done anything like that before I was about to object, to refuse to make the presentation, when suddenly a huge roar went up from the gathering,

"It's coming, it's coming."

Sure enough, round the bend of the people's road with bells ringing and whistles blowing, the gigantic black locomotive burst onto the scene. Lurching forward inch-by-inch partially obscured by massive exhausts of steam; cheers, salutations and the striking of the band welcomed the shiny steel engine. The many musical groups, that had been asked to play for the occasion, dressed in charming uniforms, gripping polished instruments, belted out several railway tunes including the favourite I've Been Workin' On The Railway. The formidable machine screeched to a halt a few feet before the end of the track and a little man called a porter jumped down onto the ground. He pulled a set of collapsible steps down from the doorway and then stood smartly at attention while the local school children began singing God Save the King, in honour of the Prince's father. William Ridley, one of the founders of the railway, greeted the many officials, commissioners, the governor and of course the Prince, as they descended the moveable stairs onto the station platform. With much pomp and circumstance and all the pageantry of a coronation, the young Prince drove in the last golden spike. A brief ribbon cutting pursued with Sir John Glover doing the honours of snipping the satin cord with a rather ominous pair of scissors. The procession then paraded to the hall, climbed up the trestle onto the make shift dais and was graciously seated and welcomed with handshakes all round.

"I won't do it!" I announced.

Bridie who rarely showed annoyance frowned down at me and said, "You will."

"I won't, I won't."

A voice boomed out, "Druscilla Soper will now bestow a token of our esteemed appreciation."

Shadrach, seeing that I was about to cause an unwanted commotion with my stubbornness, grabbed my arm and dragged me forward coaxing,

"I'll go with you. We'll do it together."

Not to be defeated in my determined refusal to participate, I dropped the spray of garden flowers and yanked a few remaining weeds at the side of the road up by their roots.

Silence fell.

I managed a curtsey and Shadrach by my side, a bow. I shoved the handful of drooping weeds under his Royal Highness' nose. Murmurings could be heard from those spectators standing closest to the platform.

The Prince spoke in a loud strong voice,

"What an adorable wee couple, the one so fair, as fair as the day and the other so dark, dark as night. And look at this, the wild carrot named after Queen Anne, who apparently won an embroidery contest to see who could produce lace as beautiful as these intricate clusters of tiny white flowers. It appears that we have all won contests today: you my delightful young elves, the men who worked the railway, this little fishing village and myself, for it is a rare occurrence that I speak without a stutter."

The prince patted us both on the head. We left the stage and joined Brigid, back amongst the audience without further incident. I figured I was in for it with my naughty behaviour but Bridie's only comment was "The devil moves in mysterious ways, he does, he does." Later we boarded the train and had a tour, observing the sleepers, the diner and observation car. It was an affair to remember and do you know, I never did ride that train.

Birthdays were a cause for celebration, with duff and gand for a special treat, which we both helped Bridie to prepare. Between the layers of pancake she put a thick coating of partridge jam and sometimes if we were very good, there was almond paste for the icing. Delicious slices were served along with tall glasses of freshly poured milk straight from our cow, Minerva. That cow of course, had been a cast off from Uncle Henry. He couldn't get her to milk. He loved to tell the story of how she had once kicked him right off the milking stool face first into a cow paddy. That was it; he tied her up with a rope around her neck and led her straight over to our place. She produced milk since that episode, pails of it, enough for our small family, any neighbours who were in need and all the visitors that came our way. We had presents too, for our birthdays, which we made in great anticipation of giving them. One year, Shadrach surprised me with a doll made out of a wooden clothes peg. Brigid had dressed it in a hand-sewn nightgown and cap while Shadrach had painted its face with a big smile. I kept that gift tucked under my pillow until this very day.

Bedtime was story time. We slept together in a hammock cuddled under a fur rug that Brigid said her father had bought from some Indian years ago. So we pretended, Shadrach was the chief and I the squaw, defending our country with bow and arrow. Or, we were hunters out to find food for our tribe who depended on us as they waited in their tents for our return. Sometimes Shadrach would talk about the children we would have when we were married, how he would protect them with his tomahawk just like an Indian warrior. And I would describe our wedding with drums beating, feather headdresses worn by all the guests and the bride and groom in beaded leather arriving on white stallions for the ceremony. Sometimes we pretended we were creatures of the ocean, he a sea horse galloping toward me, a half woman with a shiny fish tail. Anything was feasible beneath the water's surface in that aquatic land of coral castles and pink pearl shells. What wonderful imaginations we had, what moments of glory we created for ourselves. Often we fabricated a life together as a pair of swans living on Lady Lake. He the black swan, a knight in shining armour and I the white virgin, gliding together, not realizing the collision path that was about to interrupt our lives.

Blind John Soper came to visit every Sunday with Charlotte as his guide, her eyes serving them both. The four of us would sit intimately gathered about the kitchen table bowing our heads as Charlotte said the grace. What was meant to be a short blessing before the meal usually succeeded in being a lengthy prayer. As we impatiently waited for her to finish with the amens, Shadrach and I would bang our knees together hidden under the tabletop. When she finally signalled that we could began to partake of the delicious repast, which Bridie, with our help of course, had prepared, we had usually worked ourselves into a state of the fidgets. We wiggled our bottoms against the seats and laughed at Charlotte sitting properly, staring at us through squinty lids, frowning at our childish behaviour. Even then she needed glasses and I speculated that she might go blind just like our father. We listened to our parents talking animatedly about the future, our future. The opportunities they each saw for us, their expectations laid out like the Sunday tablecloth provided the entire din-

ner with an invigorating conversation. We were happy, delighting in our unison, believing that nothing would disturb our contentment. And for many years nothing did.

CHAPTER 10

Journal II
1890-1895

CHILDHOOD LOST

Unbalanced
fading,
faltering
falling,
the body bruised,
ruptured reason.
Blindness
brings rebirth.

*U*nexpectedly, Blind John decided I should go to school. He wanted something for me, which he had never had. He wanted me to get an education. I wanted to stay with Shadrach. I pleaded with Brigid to intercept on my behalf, to convince my father to let me stay with her and more importantly, with her son. There were tears. I begged that Shadrach be allowed to attend the classes with me; but that was not included in the adult scheme of things. The plan was for him to learn the fishing business. More tears.

So I went to school.

Alone.

Down the path, along the road into town.

Alone.

With tears flowing down my cheeks.

I could taste the salt trickling over my lips, but it was not the brine of the deep and no sea steed chased me. Everyday after school I would walk to Pynn Place to teach Shadrach what I had learned. Tutoring him was the happiest part of the whole school day. Just to be with him, to sit close to him, to hold his hand, to continue our journey together. I learned to read, Shadrach learned to read and still we cried over and over for the separation. I learned to write, Shadrach learned to write and still we wept for the severance that was forced upon us. Life was not the same and we started to grow up. No longer children, no longer free. We survived for the moments that we snatched in time to be together. The saddest part of every day was returning in the evening to my new home, as Blind John and Charlotte had decided that I was old enough to move back into my real home. Where they said, "You belong." Where they said, "You should be raised."

My father was a kind man. He lost his sight as a very young boy when he fell ill with a dreadful fever. After that, people called him *omadhawn and oonshick, a foolish, stupid lad. With me, he had no rules. He only guided.*

"Learn Druscilla – learn as much as you can, for as long as you can."

His sole purpose was not to segregate Shadrach and I, nor to prevent us from being together but merely to eliminate the hated name calling that he had been subjected to for most of his life. Charlotte on the other hand saw things in a different light. Charlotte always saw things differently than anyone else. By the time she had reached the quarter century mark, the puritanical purge of her mind and body had set in. She was diligent in her church going, zealous in all religious activities, faithful to a daily reading of the good book and a quotidian round of prayers. In fact, so fanatical was she to her beliefs; that only the biblical printed word was allowed in the house. Charlotte had gone to school for two years before our mother had died but following that unfortunate event she had been relegated to a domestic life of drudgery and the constant care of our father. I think she loathed her life and when I came home, she despised it even more. She never allowed herself any amusement nor any extravagance. She lived strictly by the Ten Commandments. She made it her duty to see that I too would live under the confinements of these God given rules. One time she confided in me, "I'm cursed, I am, I am." She never indulged in any pleasures of the heart because she believed that any self-gratification was really greed, standing at attention within the body. She frequently said, "I am not worthy, I am not worthy." There was a great deal of resentment and bitterness inside that head of hers. It disgorged in frequent fits of fury, flooding the air with hostility. When she was in the middle of these convulsive sessions, I would tip toe about the house trying to make myself as inconspicuous as possible so as not to irritate her nerves. I existed in constant tension, worried that I would do or say something that might cause her to create another scene. It took some doing, getting used to functioning in this atmosphere that was so completely opposite to the way I had been raised with Bridie.

Charlotte wasn't all venom. True, she didn't relish her status in life – but she did love our father. She cared for him better than any charwoman or nurse and she encouraged him to whittle. Whittling gave my father a sense of pride and a reason for being. He could take a piece of wood and make it unique, carving it into an animal, bird or Christian icon or for that matter, anything at all. He could sit amongst the shavings engrossed in his hobby for hours. People often came with requests for particular objects and my father would take rough driftwood, a fallen branch or split log and shape it creatively with tenderness, until it almost came alive. One unusual appeal came from a veteran sailor who begged my father to sculpt a likeness of his darling Newfoundland dog.

A collection of father's craftsmanship lined our windowsills and there was usually a story that went with each specimen. Although he obviously couldn't read, he would recount these stories at bedtime, holding me spellbound until I would nod off into never-never land. My favourite yarn was the one of the harbour dog, named Botswain after the canine hero who had rescued Napoleon Bonaparte from drowning, when the emperor had slipped overboard during a thunderstorm. Blind John described the Newfie as a big, black, hairy animal fondly known as the gentle giant. Originally bred as working dogs to haul heavy freight in carts or on sleds, they were also seen on the Island delivering milk and mail. Often used as ships mascots; they were trained as part of the crew to tow the fishing nets out to sea and then back again laden with the day's catch. They are able to survive rugged toil because of their thick water resistant double fur coat, their strong muscled tail which acts as a rudder and their webbed feet. The old captain's Botswain had become a celebrity in Harbour Grace, when a young mother and toddler had been walking along the wharf and the youngster had fallen into the deathly, turbulent, cold water. The child had let go of its mother's hand to chase after a bird that was pecking at some crusts of bread, which some fishermen had left strewn along the way. In his exuberance to capture the gull, the youngster had tripped and toppled over the edge into the black swell. On that particular day the current was swift, carrying the child downstream, tossing him about at an alarming pace. If it weren't for Botswain who had been sitting in the bow of his owner's boat, the young boy would surely have drowned. The massive black beast dove overboard and swam toward the bobbing body. Clenching its coat between his teeth, the dog managed to swim back to shore dragging the terrified screaming child with him. The hysterical mother had collapsed on the pier, passing out in fright. When the dog deposited her drenched son by her side, he took a wide stance and shook himself vigorously. The spray of salt water that shot off his massive hulk rained down on the woman's face and startled her out of her faint. Both the mother and child survived the ordeal unharmed. The story always ended with the recounting of the Newfoundland stamp which was issued in 1894 with the face of a Newfoundlander in all its glory on the front, commemorating the bravery of the breed. Blind John claimed that the head of the dog on the stamp was Harbour Grace's very own Botswain. He boasted too that his best carving was of that same dog. Charlotte, exhibiting her mean streak, always replied to this assertion with "What do you know, you can't even see it."

Life with my sister was a test. There were moments when I thought she loved me but then in an instant, she could turn my world upside down by over-reacting to a situation and then, I was positive that she hated me. Little by little as I began to find my place, my corner in this strange household, I came to accept the ups and downs of Charlotte's temperament and the frequent swing of her mood. When I wasn't doing schoolwork or chores about the house, I receded within the walls of my mind, imagining that I was with Shadrach. My reverie was filled with thoughts of us being together. We had a secret arrangement to meet at Lady Lake if ever either of us could slip away unnoticed. Bridie of course didn't care if we connected on the hush-hush or otherwise, but Charlotte had rules and I wasn't about to cross her path by not appearing to obey them.

Even though I hated being apart from Shadrach, Victoria Street School wasn't all that bad. I was fond of my teacher and I even made a few friends that I could sit with or play with during the morning and afternoon recesses. Our favourite pastime was amusing ourselves with a round of ' the big ship sails through the allie allie oh'. Ten or twelve of us would join hands to form a human chain, the last person leaning their arm against a post or wall to make a tunnel, which we would then all file under singing the song as we went. Then we would pass through the next link and the next, tying ourselves all up in knots. I liked this game the best as it reminded me of Shadrach and the big ship that he would someday sail on. While I was attending the school, the old hard wooden benches that we perched upon to hear our lessons were replaced with proper desks and chairs. I was very *proud of that desk and I kept it in perfect order with all my papers and my little notebook in a neat, tidy pile. Each year on December twenty eighth all the pupils sat the Annual Exam. It was quite an ordeal and I have to admit that my nerves were on edge and my stomach all a flutter. We started the day with the usual opening exercises, which included singing an appropriate hymn followed by the Lords Prayer. Then, a strange gentleman with white hair and a white beard who we had never laid eyes on before, began by examining our reading. Students from the very youngest to the oldest read a portion from their reader. The old man, who reminded me of Saint Nicholas, clapped his hands and told us that we all displayed commendable proficiency. He shook hands with our teacher and praised her for imparting to us a sound knowledge of spelling and a remarkable definition of words. Next we were submitted to a quiz on geographical matters and the history of England. Arithmetic was not forgotten as subsequently we were drilled on the multiplication tables. Finally, one by one we stood before the entire class and recited a piece, some humorous, some pathetic and some ethical, which we had prepared for the occasion. After all the protocol was completed, prizes were then awarded for exceptional progress and for good conduct. After my first year, I managed to be the recipient of a progress badge. When I took it home, Charlotte who rarely showed any pleasure in my achievements sewed the badge to my jacket pocket.*

When I was thirteen and had been living with my father and sister for three years, I came home from school one day to find Charlotte frantic.

"Father is ill, gravely ill." She cried.

In just a few hours he had succumbed to a serious sickness. Prostrate on his bed, tossing from side to side, he moaned in agony with excruciating abdominal pain. He had a roaring fever that was causing him to hallucinate and to perspire so profusely that droplets of sweat drenched the bedclothes. Weeping at his side, stroking his cheek, Charlotte admitted, "Dear God, I do not know what to do to help him."

I knew what to do. I coped the way I always did whenever I was faced with a crisis.

I ran for Bridie.

She came quickly, asking me several questions on the way.

"Where is the pain?"

"In his belly."

"On which side?"

"In the middle."

"Has anyone visited in the last few days who might have been ailing?"

I had to think about that one.

"Well, the peddler from the hollow was around, but he looked healthy enough. Oh yes, and one of the seaman from that ship that came in last week for repairs."

A very worried look took over Bridie's countenance and she picked up the pace as we hurried along.

"What do you think is the matter?"

"It could be his appendix, or he may have caught an influenza, I really am not sure." She responded, struggling to catch her breath, as we ran up a hill.

When we got to the house, Bridie as usual, was in control. She marched right into the sick room and took a good long look. Then she flung back the covers and lifted up my father's nightshirt exposing his chest, which by this time was covered in a red rash.

"This is a very serious situation." She said to Charlotte, while trying to entice my father to take a few sips of water. "Last week a ship that grounded off the coast of Labrador, came into the harbour for repairs to a hole in its hull. A few of the deck hands were reported to be afflicted with some disease. They were all young lads experiencing their first sea voyage. The rest of the crew thought that they were just squeamish from the rolling waves and incessant rocking of the ship, until their skin erupted in cankerous red sores. Doc Noseworthy, being the only physician within a wide stretch, was sent for. Upon boarding the foreign vessel and seeing for himself the extremely sad state of affairs existing in the afflicted men's quarters, he placed the ship under quarantine. The Doc is certain that the boat contains a pestilence of a very contagious nature. Unfortunately a few of the sailors had already come ashore to replenish their supplies and may have spread some germs in the process."

"Give it to me straight, Bridie, what exactly are we dealing with? Is it the Devil's Plague? Tell me the truth." Insisted my Aunt.

"Well Charlotte, there is no way to soften the news and of course it will be up to the Doctor to give a positive diagnosis, but I am so sorry to tell you that I think your father has the small pox."

"NO! It cannot be, it cannot be."

Brigid, anticipating one of my sister's mental explosions declared, "We must not waste energy ranting and raving, we won't know for sure until the pox pustules appear but this appalling malady can be beaten. If a plan of attack is put into action immediately, we can do battle against the terrible minister of death and at the same time prevent an epidemic. I will take Blind John to the abandoned shack behind Pynn Place, isolating him from contact with anyone else because this is a very transmittable condition. There, I will administer to him and we must all pray that he recovers. You, Charlotte must take all the clothing and bed linens that have touched his body and burn them. Then, all the walls and floors must be washed down with lime. We will post a white flag outside the door, warning anyone coming to visit that a very sick person has been inside."

"But, how will we get father to your shack? He is too weak to walk. Surely we cannot attempt to carry him."

"We will prepare a makeshift stretcher and Shadrach will come and help remove him."

So my father was transported lying on a canvas attached between two poles. The next morning he was covered in oozing eruptions, his breathing became very shallow and although Bridie tried everything in her power to bring down the fever, even she feared for his life. A few days later, her fear was realized and he perished, unable to fight any longer. We brought his lifeless body home where Charlotte proceeded to prepare his corpse for burial. She did everything without a single sign of any outward emotion. She washed our father from head to foot and oiled his skin. She tied a torn piece of sheet around his chin up over his head. He looked like he had a toothache. I asked her why she was doing that and she said to keep his mouth closed, until his body was cold and set. She dressed him in his Sunday best clothes, his suit and shirt and tie. She put his shoes on his feet. She refused to put coins on his eyelids to keep them shut. She said she wanted his eyes to be open when he entered heaven. When she had completed the job, she got me to help her lift him into his coffin. Then she stood with her back ramrod straight and prayed. I wanted to cry and to be consoled. Here we were two sisters, standing side by side, staring at our dead father and neither one of us shed a tear. Many of my father's friends came by to offer condolences. They put their arms around me, hugged me and told me that everything would be all right. No one touched Charlotte.

By the time my father had been interred a few other cases had developed and Doc Noseworthy had sent to St. John's for some of the vaccination serum; which was stored there in the hospital. My sister and I followed all of Bridie's instructions, scrubbing all the surfaces in an effort to disinfect them and incinerating every article in sight. For several days neither one of us waned. We managed to stay healthy until one morning I awoke to find my sheets soaked in blood. Petrified, I raced across the field and locked myself in the shack where my father had died. Charlotte, having chased after me, tried to persuade me to unlatch the door but I buried my head under my arms, covering my ears so I couldn't hear her begging, "Druscilla let me in. Let me in at once."

No amount of enticing on her part worked. I refused to let her in. I figured if I was going to die, I would do so alone and not subject anyone else to the terrible disease that had already stolen away my father. Unsuccessful at getting me to open the door, Charlotte hurried away and quickly returned bringing Bridie onto the scene.

"Darling girl, unbolt the entrance so that I can come in and help you. Please Druscilla, the Doctor has needles now that will make you better. Everyone befelled with the illness is taking the injections and immediately showing improvement in their condition."

While the women were trying to convince me to let them help, Shadrach broke in a window at the back and crept across the dirt floor on his hands and knees. Enfolding me in his arms, hush, hushing and rocking me soothingly, he pleaded,

"I love you Druscilla, you can't die, if you love me, let Bridie in, let her help."

Finally I assented, but made Shadrach promise not to leave my side. Bridie came in and felt me all over, peering here and looking there. Putting her hand to my forehead, testing for any sign of fever.

"You are not going to die Druscilla, in fact you are not even sick."

Answering the questioning confusion on all our faces, she explained, "It is your moontime. You have flowered into a woman. Now get up, we will go to the house and while you bathe in soothing lilac water, I will prepare some special cloths for you and explain the exciting cycle that you are going through."

Immediately Charlotte argued, "In God's name Brigid, do not speak of these things in front of the boy. Have you no decency?"

"That boy as you refer to him will become a man soon and he should know everything there is to know about the natural rhythm of life. There is no shame in the pulse of a woman's body. It is like the moon waxing and waning, like the ebb and flow of the tide, like thunder and rain transforming the air and atmosphere making all things new. A woman's bleeding allows for transformation, purification, newness and change. Come along now, while the fruit is ripe we will perform Druscilla's ritual."

All of this was overwhelming and perplexing but certainly I was glad to hear that I wasn't dying. I liked the idea of becoming a woman. I thought it would give me some control and allow me to make decisions. That very same day, while I was wallowing in the attention being showered upon me by Bridie and ignoring Charlotte's disgust, Shadrach himself suddenly, without warning, sickened. He developed all the tell tale signs of the dreaded disease which we thought had run its course, which we wrongly assumed had been eliminated. Immediately, Bridie went in search of the Doctor to get some of the cathartic, the serum that he had been administering to those stricken. But alas, it was finished, used up on the last victims who had arrived at the infirmary just the day before. Very quickly Shadrach approached death's doorstep. I sat alternately holding his hand, and applying cold compresses to his forehead. He writhed in torture, suffering from high fevers. He became delusional. He stared at me with glassy eyes. Whispering through cracked, parched lips he begged me not to leave him. He was going to die. I knew it. God was mean. He had taken my father and now he intended to steal Shadrach.

"Take me, take me too." I screamed as I flung my body over his.

Brigid hauled me off and sent me for more cool water. She heated her son with hot blankets and when the sweat coursed out of his pores, she swabbed him down with tepid sponges. When there was no improvement, she set off again into the village, leaving me alone with this dying thirteen year old boy who I was convinced would never grow old beside me. The bud of my youth had just transformed into a flourishing flower. But, I asked, for what? Shadrach would not live to taste the nectar from the bloom. I held his hand and tried to force the sap of energy that filled me, into his body.

"Live Shadrach, live. Live for me, live for us."

Bridie returned with scabs collected from people who had fallen ill and were now getting better. I didn't even ask how she managed to obtain them or what in the name of heaven she intended to do with them. She cut two pieces of flesh out of Shadrach's arm and rubbed the crusted scabs over his wound. Lighting two candles, she gave me one and with the other she walked about the darkened room canting, "May this room be filled with light and life." I never left his bedside for the entire night and in the morning the fever had subsided. Shadrach opened his sunken eyes and smiled. We had won. We had beaten back the devil's plague.

The epidemic was over. The guards who had been employed around the clock, to prevent anyone from entering or leaving the town, were released from duty and life returned to normal. The villagers who had retreated into hibernation to avoid the illness, ventured out, with hesitation, from the safety of their homes as though spring had already arrived. Spring, which we were always grateful for, with its purity and newness.

We grew up that year, Shadrach and I. Although I returned to live with Charlotte so that I could complete my schooling and Shadrach went out on the whale ships, it seemed as though we were stronger in our effort to remain together. In fact we were together even when we were apart.

CHAPTER 11

Journal III
1897

THE REGATTA

The silver trumpet
sounds.
Flags furl.
The wind does hurl.
Cheers leap from the shore.
Port hard the oar,
As whales race
across
the Lady's face.

Good health returned to Shadrach quickly following his harrowing brush with the minister of death. Always enchanted by ships and sailors, the wharf and the fishermen lured him, beckoned him toward a life at sea. Over the next few years, he left his childhood behind, journeyed unscathed through adolescence and entered manhood where he searched to find his rightful place in society. His first encounter with the rude world of adulthood was on Squid Jiggin Ground. They were a rowdy bunch out there. "Churlish, brass and uncultured pagans" was Charlotte's way of describing them. Their coarseness was the exact opposite to your father's gentle nature. I thought to myself that he might not survive amongst the big oafs with their vulgar ways or that worse still, being in their presence might change his softhearted temperament. Instead, the whole experience seemed to strengthen his tender character rather than weaken it.

At the beginning of the fishing season, an abundance of squid, short finned, ten armed marine cephalopods congregated in inshore waters. Dozens of mates both young and old, wearing an array of barvels and Cape Annes, went out for the catch of these wiggly, whitish molluscs. Their leather canvas oilskin overcoats protected them to a certain degree from fowl weather. By deftly moving a hook and line up and down the squid were jigged. A metal shank with twenty to forty tiny hooks was attached to the line. These hooks flashing beneath the surface tantalized the squid and they were easily snagged. Shadrach told me that the tons were eventually used as bait for cod fishing.

"Its remarkable Druscilla, remarkable that there are so many squid in the sea. Barrels upon barrels are filled."

For him, squid jiggin was an unsurpassed adventure. Since the schools of squid moved in closer to land at dusk, that's when the men donned their oilskins and boots and headed out in their dories and row boats.

Their camaraderie increased proportionately to the size of their catch and Shadrach always returned with an amazing yarn or two, about getting soaked to the neck or spattered with the squid's blue ink. As his skill grew, so did his importance amongst his cohorts. The older anglers admired his abilities so much so, that in his second season he was singled out and asked to crew on the whale ship Constance. Constance was a brig with two masts, square sails and three whaleboats. Shadrach was some proud of that ship, you'd think that it belonged to him personally. His knowledge of whaling expanded and once he was ashore, he would rattle off all the information that had been imparted to him. He told me that whale ships, which were large sailboats, were like factories, like foundries or refineries afloat; where everyone aboard was extremely industrious working long hard hours. These ships weren't fast like clippers but they were spacious and seaworthy. Many had their figureheads chopped off, following some Quaker tenet of literally obeying the commandment against graven images. Figureheads were believed by some to have placated the gods and ensured a safe voyage. The Constance's carved wooden sculpture had not been brutally effaced. It remained, a magnificent sea horse with powerful shoulders, perched on the prow of the ship, making the statement, "see my brute strength!" No storm, nor hurricane, nor treacherous gale would ever sink her. The number of crew on a whale ship depended on the number of whaleboats carried. The Constance had eighteen crew; six for each boat, along with a cooper, cook, blacksmith and steward. Whaleboats were equipped with sails, rudders, oars and paddles. The boat header was usually the captain and he stood on a narrow piece of wood anchored across the stern, handling the steering oar and commanding the boat. Shadrach's boat header was a tough bloke named Billy who the men nicknamed 'the goat'. He snorted and sweated a great deal and spat out gobs of mucus into the sea. He butted heads with anyone who dared to cross his path. Archi the harpooner pulled the bow oar up front while the remaining four crew rowed with oars. Archie was bald and according to Shadrach, had very bad teeth. The smell that oozed off of him blew aft and was pretty disgusting to the oarsmen. They couldn't plug their noses, as they needed both hands to row. Rowing the whaleboats was physically exerting and often Shadrach came home with huge blisters on his palms. Bridie soothed them with goose grease or sometimes the white of an egg and made gloves from an animal hide that she had purchased from a peddler and had kept stored in a closet in back of the kitchen. Gloves helped to protect the skin until some thick calluses formed. Life aboard the whale ship was tough. Revolting and monotonous, the food usually consisted of hard biscuits and greasy pork. There seemed to be an ever-ending supply of beans and bags of potatoes from which a variety of four legged critters escaped. Cockroaches scurried across the scullery floors. The pay was poor and Shadrach told me that each man received what was called a lay. This was really a percentage of the whole profit if a whale was caught and sold. The men had a saying, "No whale, no profit, no pay." Captains, mates and harpooners had cabins of their own, while the rest of the crew slept in narrow bunks that lined the walls of the ship. Rats, bed bugs and fleas infested the hold, so a great deal of scratching took place. If anyone misbehaved they were put in irons, or flogged or whipped. When all was quiet and no whale was sited, the men passed the time with scrimshaw, carving an artistic piece out of a whole whales tooth, or from seashells or tortoise shells. If two ships met at sea, they had a gam or an exchange visit but otherwise there were many long, boring days and nights. Sometimes stowaways were found, adding to the excitement of the day. There were mutinies, drunkenness, drownings and stories of ship's hulls being crushed by ice. Despite the tedious hours and occasional drama, Shadrach preferred his job aboard the ship to rowing, for there he got to take his turn as a lookout. Every day from sunrise to sunset the crew took turns watching from the crow's nest. Perched a hundred feet above the deck they watched for the spout caused by the whale's breath. Many a man fell to his death from the masthead as the ship rocked from side to side in the giant waves and the mast swung precariously high in the air. When the vapour plume was spotted the lookout yelled, "There she blows." Then, everyone thundered across the deck to launch the whaleboats. There was a frenzy of excitement as the crew rowed furiously towards its prey. Despite the enthusiasm and eagerness, the approach had to be controlled and quiet, as whales have very acute hearing. If the huge, unpredictable mammals sensed something amiss they could easily capsize an advancing boat, with one flip of the tale. When the small vessel was within a few feet of its quarry, the boat header would shout "give it to em" and thrust his weapon into the whale's back. The head of the harpoon was attached to a long coil of line, which was let out as the frightened whale dove below the surface, trying to escape the sharp pain of the puncture. The swooping and plummeting of the victim's massive weight churned and swelled the water, increasing the turbulence and the risk of any one of the boats keeling over into the direct path of the angry brute.

Shadrach savoured every moment of the hunt, from cast off to pulling the dead beast ashore. His favourite part of the entire escapade was what the men referred to as "the sleigh ride." Still alive, the whale swam across the surface at a clip sometimes as fast as a racing horse, towing and bouncing the whaleboat over the rolling swells with an alarming speed and stamina, despite the harpoon head imbedded in his skin. Salt spray flew into the men's faces, as the boat soared and rocketed, while the risk of capsizing increased at every turn.

At the end of his second season, the crew from Shadrach's boat decided to enter the Harbour Grace Regatta. Billie and Archie talked Shadrach into going into the race, along with a cousin of Billie's named Fred. This cousin had been in the competition before and his enthusiasm to win was transferred to the other three. In the evenings before sunset, at every opportunity, they practiced rowing. Shadrach explained, "All four of us need to be strong. Strength will help us scull faster. We need to be balanced just like a weigh scale. It won't do if one person is stronger than another. If we pull harder on one side than on the other, then we will just go in circles and we definitely won't win. We need to acquire a rhythm, so that we raise the oars at the same time and lower them at the same time. Then we will be victorious."

The very first regatta was in 1862, when two whaleboats challenged each other over a course of three miles for a twenty-five dollar prize. Since then, the event had increased in size and drew interest from many neighbouring communities. The course was changed to two and a half miles with whaleboats, gashers, dories and scull boats all participating, all vying for the coveted trophy and of course, the money. I was told it was called a purse "What do they mean by a purse?" I asked Shadrach.

"The prize money is put in a velvet satchel with a ribbon draw string at one end and then handed to the winning team at an awards ceremony after the race. Wouldn't we just love to win that purse?" He replied with such enthusiasm.

 The volunteer fire brigade had taken over hosting the regatta whose inception had been instigated by the old lighthouse keeper, Edward Oke. Many villagers thought it a real juxtaposition that Oke had met his destiny by drowning. That year of 1895, the regatta in all its splendour commenced on the twenty second of July. The day was hot. There was a slight breeze that sent ripples across Lady Lake. The sun shot down on the trees and hills, which in turn cast long shadows over the pond. These shadows camouflaged the real depth of the water and blocked out the approaching swell of waves, making the course more difficult. Sometimes, if the crest of a wave hit the bow of the boat in just a certain way, it turned off course loosing precious time to other competitors. Dressed in full uniform, their red jackets trimmed with gold braid, the firemen looked especially smart as they paraded down the main street, carrying their boats over their shoulders. They marched in unison to the start line on the shore of the Lake. There were several entry categories; single oar, double, four man, the firemen challenge and the all merchants class. The Harbour Grace band preceded the candidates along the way to encourage the gathering crowds, who lined the beach, to clap and cheer for their favourite teams. Whoops and roars went up as each team high stepped down to the waters edge. People had arrived at the site by various means of transportation. Some by horse and buggy, some in carts, others by foot while pulling wagons full of children or still others pushing baby carriages made their way to the race. Betting tents were busy, as those inclined waited in queue to spend their pennies on a wager.

 Boats all lined up for the four- man competition, were ready to be pushed into the water, whereupon the crew would jump in and begin to row. I was so excited to see Shadrach making ready for the start that I jumped up and down and hollered, "Go Shadrach, go." I had placed a little bet of my own with a few pennies that Bridie had given to me. If Shadrach's boat won the race, we might have enough money to go to the dance afterwards, which cost seventy-five cents. I really wanted to go to that dance. A big, multicoloured canopy had been erected on long poles from which vibrant, paper streamers blew in every direction when gusts of wind came up from the lake. I could just picture myself swirling about the dance floor in Shadrach's arms beneath that bright awning. Those not wanting to gamble on the races could spend their money at the many food booths scattered about the premises. Fruit pies, crubeens and an assortment of bake goods were for sale. Many families brought along their own picnics. While the race was in progression the women lit fires and boiled up big pots of turnips, parsnips and carrots and roasted chicken or rabbit over a spit. To boost the appetites, liquid refreshments flowed freely.

Someone blew the silver trumpet and it echoed out across the lake announcing the kick-off. All in unison, the men pushed their boats across the start and with one final shove, jumped in and began to row as fast and furious as their arms would pull and their straining muscles would allow. I kept my fingers crossed for the whole race. From where I stood, I could hear Archie and Billie yelling at Shadrach and Fred, "Pull, pull, harder, harder." The circuit was an upside down triangle and when the lead group rounded the first corner, I could tell that Shadrach and his gang were in third place. As enthusiasm mounted, the band played louder, adults and children encouraged the participants. I couldn't contain myself any longer so I scurried down the banks of the cliff to be at the finish line when the first boat arrived. As the winning crew pulled into shore, the musicians, who by this time were quite spirited on their drink, broke forth with the traditional tune "The Banks of Newfoundland." I saw with my very own eyes and I could not believe that it was Shadrach, Archie, Billie and Fred who had triumphantly powered across the finish line in first place. Running toward each other, Shadrach swooped me up and spun me around.

"We've won, we've won. We've won the trophy; we've won the money. We'll go to the dance!"

Dance, Druscilla, dance! Throw off your clothes be free.

Suddenly there was only white, the white lace flowers, of Umbelliferae beneath me, lifting me upwards. Only white music, whispering into my ear. The hot tender silk of white skin against me. The white stillness that shook the earth then stopped, as sweet white bees milk filled my soul. And the white stars of heaven above fell into my arms, into my waiting arms.

I am mesmerized by my mother's words in the journal. "Dance, Druscilla, dance." I am awestruck by these words, the very same words that I had heard in my dream. There is a sticky wetness between my thighs. I am aroused and think of Finn. I read on.

CHAPTER 12

Journal IV
1898 & 1900

THE BIRTH

Laboured time together

toward

a mother miracle.

Maimed.

Again and Again

in pain.

Alone

Favoured with flawless grace.

*A*fter the regatta, the field of flowers became our private haven. We stole away at every opportunity to repeat the glorious union that had occurred that day. When inclement weather, wind, rain and snow prevented intimacy with the elements, we lay inside by the fire on the shawl, its flowers a substitute for the living ones. The heat from the flames rising, like the heat beneath our skin. Flesh on flesh aglow with anticipation. Our minds had known each other since the beginning, since birth, but now we had found our bodies. Hot bodies, that ached to be touched, craved to be entered and to enter. Bowls waiting to be filled with the scented perfume of beautiful white blooms. I shouldn't be telling you these things. I shouldn't be telling anyone.

But—I can't help myself. I have to write it down my darling Anne, so that you will know what was between us. The passion we shared cannot be lost, cannot be forgotten. A hand rests in the soft place behind a knee. Energy diffuses hope and heat. Falling hair caresses the warm nape of a neck. Friction creates faith and fury. Veiled tears touch skin that sparkles from sunlight, emitting trust and torture. Honesty lies behind eyes where dreams erupt in love and lust. Now sleep comes where two together lie beneath the clouds and calm embraces songs and solace. Twisting and turning in the battle of the dance. The hooves of horses pounding on the ground and in our heads, the thunder of the cannons, while Shadrach the centurion would plunge forward with a purple lance and I, a virgin damsel, raped of all modesty. And the milk white hair and the milk white come they meshed.

I once heard Bridie telling a woman to take daucus carota seeds to prevent conception, so I stole a package from her cupboard and followed her instructions. After each visit to the fields of lace, I ground the pips with a pestle, mixed them with honey, swallowing the precautionary emulsion to avoid conceiving. Two years lapsed, endless days of thirst, quenched; hunger, satiated; greed, satisfied and urgency, always urgency. Vulnerable and at risk, an egg lay waiting until one day the sword took aim, pierced through the delicate membrane and I was pregnant. We were not sad, nor shocked, nor stressed. Quite the contrary, the pending arrival strengthened, nourished and fortified the bond that already tied our minds and bodies together. The little creature growing within my womb was a symbol confirming what we already knew, that we were meant to be together for all time.

We chose one sunny October day and walked a few miles into the town of Bristol's Hope. I wore Bridie's shawl draped like a veil over my head and a pale blue frock. Shadrach had polished his shoes and I laughed at the thought that we were eloping and he was concerned about shiny shoes. We were married by a justice of the peace. A short midget of a man named Mr. Rogers, the judge wore a black wrinkled suit and a crooked bow tie. Towering a foot above him, his wife was the witness. She let me hold a bouquet of dried flowers that she gave to every bride who pledged herself to wedded life in her presence. Mr. Rogers read the words, "Do you Shadrach take this woman to be your lawful wife?" Shadrach pulled the shawl away from my face saying, "I take Druscilla as my bride, to have and to hold from this day forward, to love and to cherish all the days of my life." "And I Druscilla do take you Shadrach as my lawful wedded husband for better for worse, for richer, for poorer, till death do us part."

We walked home holding hands and announced that we were husband and wife and soon would be a family. Bridie was happy and said that we should live at Pynn Place at least until the baby was born. She started singing old lullabies.

For Charlotte, however, we had fallen and were damned. "Get out of my house. Sinners! Sinners, you have offended the almighty. You will suffer from your wickedness" Her foul, unkind words gushed forth, burning, like the hot lava of a volcano. I gathered together my few belongings and once again made the trek across the field, only this time I thought it would be for good.

The months of my confinement were idyllic, I felt as though I was outside my body, looking at myself changing, growing. My belly bulged and when I walked, I swayed from side to side. I felt a need to record every jubilant moment of child bearing. Bridie suggested that I draw or paint, to mark each milestone of the journey of the birth. "It will help prepare you for the delivery, give you courage and insight and you will have a pictorial narrative as a reminder. My husband and soon to be father brought me a drawing tablet, some charcoal pencils and a palette. I began to sketch.

The drawings fell into trimesters just like the gestation. The first group depicted the closeness I experienced with nature, especially untamed animals and specifically with wolves. Bridie, searching and analyzing some old Celtic myths explained that wolves were intelligent, ferociously strong people in the lupine state. Only one sketch showed the wolf as an avenger in the foreground of the picture, protecting her brood from preying eyes; her lip curled above her canines, snarling with the ferociousness of an attacker. In the others, the female was always a proud possessive mother ambling and playing with her cubs, or licking their coats as they tore bits of meat from a carcass she had presented as a meal before them. These were the hours of nest building, padding the den and nourishing and it showed in my art. I contemplated the mother wolf with her babies and how fiercely protective she was. I vowed that I would be that way too.

The second collection was outlines of myself in various stages of undress. I called it my arrogant, conceited stage. Gradually a change of medium to oils took place. I gathered my brushes and paints and posed before the looking glass for self-portraits. My art now illustrated a part of my body as that of a swan. One morning I had felt particularly glamorous and before me on my easel a rare bird, a harpy took shape. The rapacious monster had a woman's face with a long arched neck. Attached to my own expanding torso were the bird's wings and claws, where arms and legs would be. In another pose I was a fetching wench, her skull adorned with ruffled feathers, affixed atop an aquiline neck. In a third, the completion of a trilogy I had felt seductive. The white trumpeter with exposed human breasts touched down upon the glass surface of some lake. Wide expansive wings stretched in an alluring encompassing gesture toward an equally grand black male. Gliding smoothly over the waters waves the black stalker pursued his mate.

We had only one mirror in the house and I spent hours viewing my *naked body, wondering whom the child within would look like. Toward the final stage of my expectant state I began to use some colour, mostly blue and white. Sky became sea, clouds transformed into ships whose prows had the bird like beaks of the swans and white sails fluffed out like plumage.*

When I first felt movement, Shadrach placed his hand on the mound that was our child and wept. Men don't weep but he did. He was different. He was a tender soldier, a champion and the hero of my heart. We pondered whether the infant would be a boy or girl.

"What will we name it?" he asked.

"John, I like John it is a good strong name, after my father."

"If it's a wee lassie, Brigid then?"

"We'll name her after Bridie but we'll call her Gael. Saint Brigid was the Mary of the Gael."

"Everyone is renamed when a child is born." Announced Bridie. "Husband and wife become mother and father, mothers and fathers become grandmothers and grandfathers, sisters and brothers become aunts and uncles, it is a wondrous process."

Birth is a blood mystery. It has its shadow side and frightening side with monsters and demons. Just a few days before delivery, I painted using red for the first time. A haemorrhage of crimson flooded the canvas. Silver spirits of light and dark swam downstream trying to reach the other side, while grotesque gargoyles laughed in the corners. One night a river of warm liquid ran down my leg. Bridie said labour had begun and she went about the house untying all the knots, an odd practise to ensure the umbilical cord would not be twisted. Then, she sat in the corner of the room rocking back and forth, arms outstretched, palms up, wailing. I rested lying on my side with Shadrach's body curved close up against mine, his hand between my legs pressing my secret place when the contractions came. With his other hand, he held his harmonica playing into the silence of my breathing, in and out, in and out. Hours went by, Bridie came out of her corner and offered sips of cool water from the well. Then she drew a huge circle on the pine board floors encircling the bed. A circle meant to envelope our little family in love. I asked for my sketchpad and drew a small circle with a ship at its centre. After each tightening, which gripped me at the breastbone and went all the way to my groin, I drew another circle surrounding the first. Inhaling, exhaling, panting, I blew into the sails and the ship moved ever so slowly mounting the crest of waves and floating down into the troughs. Shadrach prepared a bath and I lowered my swollen body into the copper tub. He sponged my arms and back and the trickles of warmth running over my skin, soothed my soul. The searing pains became close and harder. I rose out of the water just like the mermaid in the last sketch I had drawn before parturition. The hands on the clock moved forward ticking.

Bridie's hand shoved deep —"Ah yes, soon, now, soon.

Ticking. Wailing. Bleeding. Blowing. Knees bent. Straining. Tissue lacerated.

A tiny head emerged, wide eyes astounded. Captivated wide eyes stared and waited.

A perfect mouth, without a sound.

And then, the body.

The grandmother received the infant slowly, gently without tearing.

"Dear God what has happened?"

The little arms and legs twisted, malformed hands and feet, a heaving chest and there protruding from the crooked spine was a bulbous ugly protuberance, which was criss- crossed with hideous blue veins. From somewhere I could hear Bridie cooing to this anomaly that was our daughter, "There my child, there my Gael, see your Mother and your Father, see your Grandmother. You are loved." She quickly bound the crippled limbs with the white shawl and put the babe to my breast where amazingly she sucked with vigour.

One month, she lived one month.

There was no explanation.

Bridie, rationalizing, alleged it was the Devil's plague. Charlotte, unforgiving, claimed it was God's will, his judgement cast upon us. She drew Shadrach outside and spoke to him for a long time. Nothing was the same. Nothing would ever be the same. We grieved each in our own corner staring into the empty circle.

We went one last time and lay amongst the lace.

"I love you Druscilla. Dance for me."

Then without warning, without farewell, he left.

There was no explanation.

Everyone had an opinion. Bridie said he needed time. Time to heal. "He needs to be alone Druscilla, to recover from this terrible tragedy. In time he will return."

This explanation didn't make any sense. He had never needed to be alone before. We had always faced adversity together. Scathingly Charlotte announced "He only married you under the circumstances. Since the circumstances have been removed, the fool has reneged on his vows and left. You are better off alone." She admonished. "He's gone fortune hunting. A fool and his dreams gone off in search of land and riches."

I hated her and her abhorrent ideas.

His chums on the dock thought perhaps pirates or bucanneers had kidnapped him. Maybe some American explorers enticed him to become a soldier.

I couldn't explain it to myself nor to anyone else. I just knew that something was terribly, terribly wrong. Your father left without an explanation. Unknowingly, he hadn't really left me alone. He left me with another child growing in my womb. Nine months later you were born. Perfectly formed. I named you Anne after the flower you were conceived upon, after the ship your father departed on and after Saint Anne. I used my blue wedding gown as linen for the cradle and you lay swaddled in its folds. I was a mother. Bridie was enchanted. Charlotte granted clemency.

In the box are the drawings and sketches. I looked at each one and pressed them to my breast. There is one, only one that my mother had not mentioned in her journal. I knew for certain that it was the one she drew when I was born. A woman lying in the birth position, a long red stream flowing from between her legs across the page to wrap around the infants head, in a burst of flaming crimson hair.

The blood mystery.

CHAPTER 13

Journal V
1900-1907

ALONE

Alone
half souls.
Together
shared shadows.
Apart
decided demise.

I caressed the final journal. Inside this journal were the last words my mother had left for me. I looked again at her photo. I admired the woman, the loveliness of her. I wondered at the female uniqueness of her. I remembered the soft silken skin, the flaxen hair framing her tiny face. How to classify her beauty? This was not a rough peasant woman, nor a woman of queenly bearing. Her demeanour was quiet and serene. Although she appeared to have a certain delicacy, there also arose from her a convincing strength, like that of a tree's strong branch. I longed to be that woman: a poet, an artist, a lover, and a mother. I longed to be inside her skin, to feel her heart thumping against my ribs, to love as she had loved.

Out of the water rose a mermaid. The mermaid was called Druscilla. A shadow passed over her and she became woman. This shadow called Shadrach shed his skin and was lost. The black swan was frightened away by the baby's first wails. The white swan was deserted; abandoned, facing a great void.

Only a few letters arrived and then nothing.

I had you, my innocent one, Shadrach's perfect daughter. You came easily into the world. I loved you with all the tenderness that a mother can give. But, my heart was severed. There was a laceration so deep it would not mend. Day by day the life seeped out of me and my pulse slowed. I was dying. For your sake I tried to live. I tried to recover from my malady. I prayed. I searched for the part of me that had been lost. I begged for the return of the other singleness, which would make me whole again. I waited. I waited for seven years. Sometimes I honestly believed that Shadrach was dead. That would explain it. That would explain not a single word. Then I supposed that he was alive but maimed. I hypothesized that some terrible tragedy had befallen him and that he was unable to contact me or send me a message. When I was in the depths of despair, I lost my faith, my trust in him and I assumed that he had found another. I understood that he had simply forgotten me. On good days I was certain that he would return and that my half soul would become whole and I would recover. On those days, those good days, I took you, my wonder child and sat vigilantly watching for hours the horizon. Scanning the panorama of the open sea for my chieftain on his white horse, I waited rapturously.

Bridie did what she could to ease my trauma. In my weakened condition she encouraged me to sketch, applauding my paintings, and constantly prompting me to derive energy from the murals in my mind. She urged me to participate in the upbringing of my sprightly child. Charlotte claimed Shadrach's disappearance was all for the best. I could see, that she had set her sites on you my sweet Anne. She pampered and praised you. She hovered protectively over you, as though she were your mother and not I. Juice squeezed from a lemon compared to the vile bitterness I felt. Malicious emptiness made me angry with everyone. My sister's attitude heightened my grief and increased my concern for you. Upon my death I worried what would become of you. Who would take care of my cygnet? Bridie was aging and perhaps would not even outlive me. I thought of her remaining brothers, elderly men with aloof wives. None of them presented as very good candidates to take on an active budding youngster. I considered Delilah, childless Delilah. Bridie's sister, so different from her, living in a big city, leading a strange existence. I didn't want you to be taken away from your home, your familiar surroundings, to be shipped like an orphan to a foreign destination. Delilah, I decided, was not really a wise choice either. That left Charlotte. Obviously she loved you. For some unknown reason she treated you differently than she had attended anyone else, especially me. You brought out the best in her. But, to ask her to be your keeper was more than I could face. As the light within me dimmed, and Shadrach grew further and further away, you my child, glowed. As my strength ebbed, your vitality increased. It was only when you grasped my finger with your little hand that I felt the presence of another one so dear – the omnipresent presence that never left me.

There were moments when I had a notion to take you with me to a high cliff and then leap off, the two of us together, floating on a draft of air down, down into the pool of water where all sea creatures return to. Down where Shadrach must be with the mermaid. One day I decided to do just that. With Shadrach's baby shawl, I made a sling around my neck and rested you in the hammock like a pouch; in that way my arms would be free. When I reached the summit of the rocky precipice, I stood on the very edge and raised my arms up toward the sky like a mammoth butterfly about to take flight. The waves were crashing against the shore below, the wind was hurling about my feet, your child fingers were caught in the network of the shawl and you began to cry.

It was you Anne; it was you who cried out. It was you who saved me from that death-defining hurdle.

One night there was a big celebration. I think it might have been Guy Fawkes Night because there was a bonfire in a neighbour's field. People were dancing and singing. Taking you by the hand, we walked together across the meadow to join in the festivities. I could hardly catch my breath. I felt weak. It was an effort to push one foot in front of the other. The earth beneath my feet was sucking out the energy from me as I barely managed one step forward and then another. I became weaker and weaker. When we arrived the fire fascinated me. Still gripping you by the hand, I drew closer and closer to the intensity of the blaze. It looked like the earth was erupting, heaving up hot lava. Someone was dancing inside the flames. I heard my name, "Druscilla, Druscilla, dance for me." I could feel the heat on my face, my body.

Then-

"Mommy, mommy."

It was you Anne; it was you who cried out. It was you who stopped me from jumping into the fire, from being burned at the stake like Fawke's effigy.

I didn't have the courage to leap off the cliff. I didn't have the strength to walk into the fire. I thought about hanging myself from a tree. I considered drinking a cup of poison. I might have shot myself if I could have found a pistol. It was after these morbid thoughts that I made the decision to ask Charlotte to be your guardian. Seven years I thought about death. If Shadrach was dead, I wanted to die. If Shadrach lived, I too wanted to live.

But I didn't know his fate. There was so much I didn't know.

My mother didn't kill herself. Like a tree, which cannot get enough sustenance from the earth, she just withered away. Her nourishment came from my father. When he wasn't there to feed her, she died. She lay down in the hammock with the white shawl pulled over her body and died.

CHAPTER 14

1919

THE DISCOVERY

Truth
weaves patterns,
mapping out
a turbulent sea.
Tells
secrets of passion,
revealing
rites of passage.

In that year of 1919 we eagerly awaited the arrival of Imbolc. The Celtic year is divided into light and dark, Imbolc signifying light, life, the promise of spring and new beginnings. Finn cherished all Irish traditions but Imbolc he told me was his favourite.

"Why?" I asked. "Why is that your favourite?"

"Every year for hundreds of years around the time of Imbolc, the seat of the kingship of Ireland was burned to the ground. Every year the King's overseers and workmen attempted to rebuild the dun only to have it reduced to ashes again and again. It came to be, that one year the King announced he would give his only daughter to any man who could save the Kingship from the fire goblin. Hundreds of warriors and would be suitors of the princess attempted unsuccessfully to defend the King's land. Defeated, they were imprisoned in the castle dungeon. The King's fury over his losses multiplied. Living in the forest outside the King's property was my ancestral idol, the young Fionn MacCumhail. He overheard the forest people talking about the King's proclamation and said, "I will save the King's domain for the sake of the daughter." And that's exactly what he did. Thereafter the fire goblin was never to be seen again. Victorious, MacCumhail became a hero and champion over all of Ireland. True to his word the King gave him his daughter's hand. Fionn would not accept the prize. Instead he asked that the prisoners be set free from bondage. Thankful for all that the white haired soldier had done, the King honoured his wishes and freed the men. They came out from the darkness of captivity into the light of Imbolc. They praised the man responsible for their release and became his followers. They were the first Fenians. And that my love is why I cherish Imbolc."

"It 'tis a great story, it 'tis, it 'tis. In these parts, Imbolc is known as Candlemas and February is often referred to as the wolf month. I look forward to the first day of February because it is Shadrach's birthday and the festival of Saint Brigid. As the old woman of winter melts into the past, Brigid is reborn as the young bride of spring. With her white wand of light she opens eyes to the tears, smiles, sighs and laughter of the seasons rebirth. So you see Finn, I too am connected to Imbolc."

Our first February together brought the earliest whisperings of spring. An exceedingly warm air current conveyed the virgin bride in over the harbour and delivered Imbolc to us. Patches of snow began to soften when struck by the first rays of the morning sun. In those flowerbeds sheltered by crumbling, stone walls, white crocus soaked up the sun's heat and popped up through the earth's hard crust. It was a day so rich with the promise of new beginnings that it lured lovers out into the fresh clean air, to stroll down country lanes. We were in love now, Finn and I, seizing every opportunity to touch, to kiss, and to hold each other close.

Who knew?

Not Charlotte, not Oisin, no one.

Only we knew.

We guarded this knowledge, preferring to take hidden pleasure in our hopes and dreams for the future. We took enjoyment in our physical attraction and delight in the emotional growth of our relationship – a relationship that had yet to be consummated.

I had confessed cautiously to Finn about my mother's box, revealing to him its entire contents. Gambling on what his response might be, I divulged my plan to travel to Boston in search of my father. Thankfully, he was understanding and supportive. He even insisted on helping me pay for the ticket.

"The sooner you do this, the sooner you can return to me. I am selfish. Now that I have met you, I want you by my side all the time. I don't really want to let you out of my sight but I know that it is important for you to make this trip. You should go this summer. I would go with you but I think that this is something you must do on your own."

As much as I wanted to have him beside me, to help me find my way, I knew he was right and that this was my task. I knew, to find the past, I must go unaccompanied, unhampered by the trappings of the future. Finn had settled nicely into Pynn Place and had easily slipped into Bridie's role of tending to the ill and downhearted. What was supposed to have been a few months stay, a vacation with his Grandfather, appeared to be turning into a permanent arrangement. I thought of him as my very own hero, not unlike the legendary Fionn MacCumhail. He had rescued me from the confining doom of Charlotte's custody. Once when entangled in his powerful embrace, I asked if he intended to stay in Harbour Grace.

"Do you want me to stay?" He had asked, while stroking my hair and looking directly into my eyes.

I wanted him to stay but for some reason I couldn't bring myself to admit it.

"I will stay for as long as you need me." He promised, as our bodies became more involved and more increasingly entwined.

With spring came Mr. Webber. He arrived one afternoon for his annual visit in a shiny black 1917 Model T Ford. What excitement that stirred as he drove into town from St. John's over the bumpy ruts and furrows on the only road that was remotely passable to an automobile. Beeping his horn to announce his approach and waving his hand like royalty to passers-by, as he motored down the main street, young children and many adults fell in behind the car to follow him along the way. So new and unfamiliar was this modern creation that everyone wanted a peek. Mr. Webber pulled up in front of P & P's. Having been on the same ship The Sea Soldier, as his dear friend Edward and the two sisters and having survived the marauders vicious attack, he journeyed every year from Boston to see his old chum's daughters. Mr. Webber was a goldsmith and gemologist of the utmost talent. Following the buccaneer's ambush of the fated ship, he had carried on with his plans to open a fine jewellery shop in America's great seaport. Climbing out of the drivers seat, he stood poised for a moment with his hand resting on the curve of the huge polished fender, allowing the curiosity seekers to take a good look. His dazzling comportment prevented those timid of nature from coming forth but the most boisterous of the group approached with a myriad of questions about what was to them, quite a foreign mode of transportation. Attired in fashionable driving garments, the man clearly enjoyed being the centre of attention. He told the crowd that he affectionately called his coup Tin Lizzie and boasted, that he had paid three hundred and sixty American dollars for it. He caressed the headlights with his gloved hand and waved his arm across the grill which had the gleaming, gold letters of Ford written on it. For those men who were really mechanically inclined, he showed them the four cylinder, twenty-horse power engine and even let them climb up into the cab to observe the two speed foot pedal which controlled the transmission. Even I was impressed with the folded plait upholstery on the front and rear seats and the little shade curtains covering the rear side and back windows. Having exhibited the car for what he considered an appropriate length of time, the gentleman tapped his kid-skinned gauntlet with the ivory handle of his walking stick and the four of us proceeded into the millenary and up the stairs to the sisters' living quarters. The two women doted on their guest, making sure he was comfortable in a high backed green leather armchair. They tucked a stool beneath his feet and silk encased pillow behind his head, while offering afternoon tea. Mr. Webber relished their attention and exhibited his appreciation by showering them with favours, which he had brought from his establishment in Boston. Matching tortoise shell hair combs, one for each of "my darlings" as he referred to the women, seed pearl bracelets and crystal drop earrings for both of them. As he talked about his plans to broaden his horizons and open a boutique in New York, his handle bar moustache wiggled up and down and his eyebrows arched in anticipation of this new adventure. Finally, when it appeared that he had finished recounting all that had transpired since his previous visit, Phoebe appealed to him for some assistance on my behalf in the matter of the hat pin.

"Dear friend, several months ago, our young clerk here brought to us a magnificent hat pin which had belonged to her grandmother. Prudence and I wondered if you would be so kind as to examine it. We think that it is quite a valuable piece and we would welcome your opinion on the subject."

"My darlings, I would be honoured to inspect the pin. Bring it to me and I shall consider its origin and worth."

Taking the pin from its box, I handed it over, thinking that the truth of its value was about to be exposed. After several moments of contemplation and viewing the piece from a number of angles with a magnifying glass, a long, soft whistle came forth from his lips.

"It is indeed remarkable. How did you say it came to be in your possession?"

"It was my grandmother's, given to her apparently when her son, my father, was born." I replied. Not in my wildest imagination did I comprehend where the information, which I was about to hear, would lead.

"Well, this is a genuine work of art. Originally it was a royal brooch, that is to say it belonged to Queen Anne of England. She commissioned its fabrication back in the late 1600's about the time when her ninth child was conceived. The Queen was well known for her talent of crocheting elegant shawls. She had the brooch fashioned in the design, which she liked the most. See, here at the centre is a perfectly cut amethyst, the most prized type of quartz, surrounded by these nine petals each with nine miniature diamonds. Amethysts are said to dissipate evil thoughts and quicken intelligence, they vary in colour from a lovely light lilac to a deep royal purple like this one. These are not diamond chips, but perfectly cut, flawless gems and of the utmost quality."

Rubbing his hands together in glee, he announced, "Oh yes, at auction this would bring a very substantial sum of money, enough for you and your children to live on for the rest of your lives. Interestingly, the Queen was purported to have given the ornament to a suitor, a paramour if you will. Thereafter, the man left England for America, arriving in New Orleans where he sold his valuable possession. Of course, this palatial courtesan was unable to provide any documentation on the jewel's legitimacy but took what monies he could and left. The new owner, a very famous craftsman from London who at this point was living on Royal Street in New Orleans proceeded to secure papers on its genuineness. After receiving a certificate of authenticity, he used his intriguing artistic talent and turned the brooch into a hatpin, keeping it as part of his wealth for many, many years. It was rumoured that he eventually sold the item but no one knew to whom. How your grandmother came to be the owner is a very mystifying question indeed. Who was it that gave it to her, do you know?"

I told Mr. Webber, that I had no idea who it was that had made my grandmother the recipient of the pin. But, in the recesses of my brain, an inkling of suspicion, and a fragment from a document came forward. It was a clue I wasn't sure I was prepared to accept. Not wanting to appear rude, I sat and endured the remainder of the conversation, the entire time thinking only of getting home and doing some detective work. As soon as it was possible, I thanked Mr. Webber for his expert opinion and excused myself on the premise that my Aunt was waiting for my return, which for once was really not true. I raced home as fast as I could and got out the will, Bridie's will. Sure enough, my sleuthing verified the theory growing in my head. There it was in black and white. "Oisin Sweetapple, formerly of New Orleans, dearest friend-----." I pondered this statement. If Finn's grandfather was from New Orleans and the hatpin came from New Orleans and he was the dearest friend------the whole idea was unthinkable.

For the second time that day I packed up the pin in its felt lined box but this time I headed straight for the manse. I prayed that Oisin would be alone, so that I could question him without Finn in attendance and I hoped that there would be a plausible explanation to these incredible coincidences.

The Reverend greeted me good naturedly, as was his custom.

"I've come to you about a very grave situation that has just this day been brought to my attention. It is of the utmost importance that I address this issue with you, to ease my state of mind." I said to him

"And what might this urgent matter be?"

I held out the hatpin, in a gesture that he should take it, watching to see what kind of reaction, what emotion I might have aroused. A look of concern settled about the creases around his eyes. The shadows of dusk flickering in through the windows descended upon him like a pall. His trembling fingers touched the precious stones and the silence that lay between us was like a gaping wound, bleeding out the truth.

"Did you give this to Brigid?" I asked.

He confessed, "Aye child, I did."

"Did you give it to her on the day my father was born?"

"I did, I did." He whispered, with a note of passion in his utterance. Closing his eyes, he held the pin to his heart, where it seemed to ignite the flames of memory. Visibly shaken, by my abrupt approach, my intrusion on his privacy, he spoke.

"Where to begin, where to begin? I can certainly appreciate that you are not to be dissuaded in your search for answers to questions that should have been addressed a long time ago. Come, sit by my side and I will tell you about Brigid and myself.

Once many years ago, I made her a solemn promise, a pledge, that I would never reveal our story to anyone and I have kept that vow until now. But you have the hatpin and you have discovered at least a part of the truth, am I not correct?"

I nodded.

"What does it matter, if I breach that oath now? Brigid is gone and I am an old man. Someone should know the facts and it should be you. Your grandmother encompassed three women; liken to her namesake the triple goddess. She embodied the maiden of purity and innocence, the mother of comfort and fruitfulness and the crone of wisdom and healing. When she was in her prime, the second stage of her life, her desire to have a child was beyond comprehension but unlike most women she did not wish to marry. In that way she was also like her namesake. She went hunting; on the prowl like a wolf to find its prey, to find a mate. I was the quarry. One day I was walking along the escarpment when a strange and blinding fairy mist moved in from the sea. As the mist dispersed itself outward, Bridie appeared in its midst captivating my attention with her flaming red hair falling about her shoulders and over her long dark cape.

"Shaman, shaman." She called out to me.

"How can I be of service to you?" I asked. Thinking that she was looking for a man of God.

"I have come to take you home with me. I have chosen you to be the father of my child."

She was enchanting, weaving her way back and forth in front of me and her words enticed. In essence, she seduced me and I must admit, I allowed myself to be seduced. Desperately unhappy with my own situation in life, I succumbed. My first indiscretion, one of two transgressions and I have suffered silently, secretly ever since. I have not suffered because I sinned; I suffered because on that day I fell in love. I fell in love for the first time. I fell in love with a woman who became a phantom of my thoughts. I fell in love, but my love was not reciprocated. After that affair which fulfilled Brigid's need to become a mother, I returned to my real family and my post in New Orleans. I have often reasoned that I allowed myself that fall from grace because of the mental anguish, which I endured trying to satisfy a bible thumping father, a wife to whom I was a nuisance and a son I could not relate to. But these are only rationalizations.

The reality was I desired Brigid Pynn. I longed for her beyond my wildest imagination and that is the truth. Determined that the world should not be privy to whom the father of her child was; she insisted that I keep my distance. She was resolute that I stay away from her. She told me that if I could not feel affection for my wife and devotion for my other child, to seek it elsewhere. She said, "Look on the hills, look in the valleys. You have done me a great service and I know that one day, love will come to you. Now go and do not return."

I defied her only once and that was when I returned to Harbour Grace for the birth of her son, my son, our son. I yearned to hold both the child and the mother in my arms one last time before I donned the cloak of anonymity. I wanted to give this child something. I needed for my own peace of mind to leave with him a token of my love. I became a hermit burrowing myself away, devoting hours upon hours researching the perfect gift; one that would be the most meaningful and that would leave a lasting impression.

During my pursuit of this article of perfection, I uncovered the legend of the amethyst from ancient Greece. Being a poet and romantic by nature, this intrigued me and I saw myself in the myth. Dionysus the god of intoxication (certainly I had been intoxicated by Brigid) who had a vicious temper was angered one day and swore to take revenge on the very next person to cross his path. He created fierce tigers (or could it have been wolves) to carry out his vindictiveness. An unsuspecting young maiden named Amethyst was the first to walk before the angry Dionysus and his beasts. The goddess Dianna wanted to protect Amethyst from the brutal claws of the animals so she turned the virgin damsel into a statue of pure crystalline quartz. Dionysus who had instantly fallen in love with the maiden began to weep tears of wine in remorse for his terrible temper. The tears stained the statue purple creating the gem we know today. Diamonds, to the Greeks, also represented the tears of the gods. To the Romans they were the splinters from the stars, which Eros used for the tips of his arrows. Today diamonds have come to personify the unbreakable bond of love between a man and woman.

Having unearthed these facts I purchased the hatpin, which so artistically combined both amethyst and diamonds and which I believed represented the love and affection I held for Brigid and my son. One afternoon during my daily wanderings of old Orleans I had come upon a curiosity shop and spotted the pin in its window. It was the unusual shape and the fact that it reminded me of lace that sealed my desire to purchase it. I ravaged my savings and left my wife and Oscar my son, bereft of any financial security. I can see by the expression on your face that you are shocked. Believe me, all of those around me at that time were taken by surprise by my unpardonable actions – actions that left everyone doubting my sanity.

When I arrived back here in Newfoundland for the birth, I went straight to Pynn Place. There in a wooden cradle lay my son swaddled in the shawl that he had been conceived on. He looked at me with his dark brown eyes and smiled. I put the golden stem of the pin into his little hand and he clenched it within his tiny fist. Brigid was enraptured and I had been blessed with a strong healthy baby, who did not bear the mark of Finn Sweetapple, for he had black curly hair and a dusky complexion. I knew for sure that His father would not decide His destination and in this respect, history would not repeat itself. I left that same day for home, determined to make amends with my spouse and my other son for having stripped them of all my assets. Never cognizant of the truth behind my bankruptcy, my wife was nevertheless unforgiving. Had I told her of my liaison and resulting offspring, she would have left and taken Oscar with her. Instead I paid dearly for my wickedness as she continued to abide in the same house, frigid and unforgiving. I do not believe that Shadrach ever knew that I was his father. Brigid certainly never told him—and I? I never travelled this way again until my later years when I was assigned this parish in my retirement and by that time he had vanished. Brigid sent infrequent letters announcing the milestones in his life but beyond those, I never knew my son.

Now Anne Pynn, you know the story and you also know that I am your grandfather."

Confusion reined in my head. Finn and I shared the same grandfather. What relationship did that make us to each other? Definitely we were close, too close. Suddenly I was faced with the idea that intimacy between us would go beyond the boundaries of what was acceptable by law. Both the Bible and legal codes refuse to sanction marriages of close relatives. I heard the words, "Does anyone see just cause?" and "Speak now or forever hold your peace!"

Resounding in my ears. I hated to imagine what would happen if Charlotte were ever to become privy to my discovery. I cringed at what the results of such a union might bring. Horrible pictures of children with deformities or worse still imbeciles crawling around on all fours passed before my eyes.

"Do you know where he is, my father?" I asked. The trembling question forced out through an emotionally constricted throat.

"No lass, that is something I do not know."

"What about Finn?" I was in tears. "What in the name of heaven will I ever tell this man, who is your grandson, who has fallen in love with your granddaughter?"

Taking a handkerchief from his pocket, he dabbed at the drops assaulting my cheeks. "Tell him? Tell him everything, or tell him nothing. In confidence I have laid bare my soul, disclosed my sorrow and my joy; it is now up to you to speak or be silent. It is said in this country that a child born who never sees his father, inherits the power. Shadrach had that force and so do you my daughter. You have the power to annihilate or to begin again."

I left.

I left with a power that I wished I had never received.

I left taking with me the object responsible for disclosing the truth. Now I had three reasons for going in search of my father. To give him the hat pin, to let him see living proof that he had a normal healthy daughter and to tell him who his father was. This knowledge that I held within me, and the ramifications of divulging it was building up inside me like a hot fireball ready to explode. Building up, like a volcano ready to discharge, spewing out hot damaging liquid. Building up, like the heat of a bon fire on Guy Fawkes Day. I couldn't wait all those weeks till the summer. I would go as soon as I could arrange my voyage.

CHAPTER 15

1930

PYNN PLACE

A Haven
A home
A heaven
A hell,
with doors
of secrets
walls of comfort
and
windows of delight.

As I recollect those two years from 1918 to 1920, I think of how Bridie left her past in Pynn Place. How my mother left her past in a box. I will leave my past in this book. I do most of my writing in my office, looking out on Lady Lake. The calm green waters inspire my literary skills. The walls of Pynn Place keep me safe and secure and motivate me to keep writing of those long ago years. I can look down from my third storey window and see the old house. Bridie's house where it all began, where Shadrach was born, where my mother spent most of her childhood years, where in fact I was born and where I gave birth to Belle. It hasn't changed much; the well is still in the front yard and if I close my eyes I can imagine Bridie standing on the porch waving to an approaching stranger, beckoning them with open arms of comfort. Since we built our own home on Oisin's land, Pynn Place is the pivot of all the activity that takes place throughout the entire complex. It houses the administration offices and is the portal of entrance to our other facilities. From my lookout, I can see across the slope of our main floor roof jutting out from beneath the second floor eaves, offering a panorama of Charlotte's land on the other side. There is a full view of a white framed structure, the building known now as Lace House, a secluded haven for young girls whose families have disowned them and for women who have so many children, they don't know what to do with another one. There are many families in Newfoundland that have twelve to fifteen children and the mothers go nearly frantic when they find they are pregnant yet another time. Both the unwed girls and saturated women can discreetly give birth at Lace House; knowing their secret will be kept within its walls and their babies will be placed with a loving adoptive family.

It was Charlotte's last wish that we incorporate her property into the rest of Pynn Place and that we create a refuge for women. After much consideration and deliberation the decision was finalized. I think if she were still with us, she would be satisfied with what we have achieved and even feel some exoneration. Behind our house is Deer Inn, the newest structure and first out-building of the complex. From my North window I can see the smooth simple line of its architecture, the comings and goings of the staff, the Inn's curious wee inhabitants and our gardener, weeding and pruning the flower beds and herb gardens.

I remember that day when the plans were formulated, the day I returned from Oisin Sweetapple with my unspeakable discovery locked inside my head. I walked past that well where water had been drawn to soothe the parched lips of my mother while she laboured giving birth to her first child. I creaked up the tumbledown steps, the same ones that Tommy Three had hastily ascended to announce the loss of our beloved Bridie. I entered the room where so many infants had been brought into this world, red faced and screaming. There was a new masculine feel about the house, since Finn had moved in. Even the smell was different. There was still an assault on the senses as one walked across the threshold of the porch into the kitchen but now it was the sweetness of pipe tobacco, the pungency of a man's sweat and the masking whiff of cologne; where before it had been lavender, spices, the muskiness of femininity, fresh earth and birth. Combined with his natural born healing abilities and his educated medical ones, Finn had continued where Bridie's hand left off. With expertise and compassion he administered to the sick and offered shelter and food to the needy. On that day of revelation, he stood waiting for me, leaning against the veranda railing, inhaling from his pipe, the bowl cupped in his hand the stem clenched between his teeth. As it often did in those days, my imagination played games and my own inner voice tricked me, "he's a phantom, a ghost dressed in white pants, a white fisherman's sweater, with white hair and white smoke enveloping him."

I had a notion that I was in another world, a secret dream world where my discovery and its validity had not materialized and the resulting events had not occurred, had not happened to me. I thought if I pinched myself I would wake up from the preposterous situation. I'd be just me, Anne Pynn, seller of hats. The hug Finn gave me was real enough, as he asked half in jest, "Is it good news, is the pin worth a fortune?"

I acquainted him with the pin's historical background, deceivingly omitting the part about Royal Street, and told him what Webber had suggested its value to be. I stared into his eyes thinking, 'we share the same grandfather and I am not going to tell him. I'm in love with this man, we have a future together and I am not going to reveal the hidden familial ties. Our friendship, our newfound devotion is too young, too tender and with his religious background, he might decide that it would be immoral to continue. Anyway if the Reverend didn't see fit to tell him, then far be it for me to be the one to break the news. If I go now to New England, we'll be apart for some time and it will give me a chance to think about the fair, the just, the honourable thing to do.' Choosing my words carefully I told him,

"I have this duty to find my father. It's a task I've set for myself which hangs over my head like an ominous black thundercloud. It blinds me from performing my normal duties. It obscures my ability to think clearly or participate in any other activity wholeheartedly. In fact, my heart is so heavy with this responsibility that I don't think I can wait till summer to go to Boston. I think I should leave as soon as possible. I'm going to need assistance, gathering my belongings for the trip, telling Aunt Charlotte, will you help me make the arrangements?"

Finn obviously not prepared for this request, responded slightly aggressively, showing on his part, a possessiveness toward me that hitherto had not been apparent.

"I can't let you do this by yourself. How will you know where to go? Boston is too big a city. Many strange inhabitants walk the streets and are threatening to a young woman travelling around alone. I'm concerned for your safety. You've never been anywhere outside of Harbour Grace, you can't just land there without some kind of plan, some course of action with which to begin your search."

"The few letters which my father sent to my mother all had the same return address, The Arcadia House Lodge. I know that was eighteen years ago and a lot could have happened since then, but it's a place to start. What I will do, is go on the Caribou into St. John's and arrange to stay a few days with my great aunt Delilah. In fact, I have already notified her by post of my intentions. She was Bridie's younger sister and I know she would be more than happy to have me as a guest in her home."

"The Caribou, what are you talking about, the Caribou?"

"That's the train, I forgot, you wouldn't know it by that name. Anyway, while I have a visit with Delilah I'll go to the port and purchase the steamship tickets. Perhaps I could even travel on a schooner. I'd like that, I'd feel as though I were tracing my father's footsteps."

Taking my hand Finn spoke with great sincerity.

"I've only just discovered you. I want you for myself. Maybe we could come to a compromise and I could go with you as far as St. John's. Would you like that?"

"Let me think about it."

"Right, then you think about it, but don't think too long or too hard. Now let's take a walk about the property. I have some plans that I want to tell you about. Get a jacket, so you won't catch a chill. Come along now, don't be tardy."

We trod that day the entire length of Lady Lake while Finn revealed his plans.

"My grandfather is giving me the land which Bridie left to him. He and I have had a discussion about the dire straits that the local hospital is in and he wants me to take the land and use it to build modern medical facilities, possibly a hospital or sanatorium or at the very least a clinic. You know the number of people that come to Pynn Place for help has steadily increased over the years and it really needs to be expanded. I think Bridie would be in favour of this project, don't you?"

"Your grandfather is just giving you the property, just like that?" I asked cautiously while thinking – this is my grandfather too. What in the name of all that is sacred, I wondered, was Oisin doing trying to bring us together through the land, while at the same time knowing that we had fallen in love.

"Well you must remember he was Bridie's dearest friend and she his closest confidante. She was always noted for her generosity to the sick and the poor. He just thought this would be a good way to honour her memory and at the same time satisfy my desire to remain here in Harbour Grace. Besides, he knows he is getting old and might not be around too much longer; he wanted to do something while he was alive and still able to make sound decisions. You know he told me a peculiar story about St. Brigid. He said that when she was seeking land for her community she asked the King for only as much as her cloak would cover. Which of course would be just the tiniest parcel yet miraculously her cloak spread over the whole curragh. In a sense that's what Bridie's land will do. If you and I bring these plans to fruition; it will develop to serve the whole community."

"But Finn, you and I to do this? You assuredly are a competent, capable physician but I am hardly qualified to be of any assistance. What would I do?"

"You could go back to school and learn to run a business. The whole idea might sound preposterous but I know we could do it. We could do it together."

"It sounds like a lifetime commitment." I replied with apprehension and fear.

"It is that, Anne Pynn, it is that. And we will be partners, partners for life."

Suddenly he blurted out, "Will you marry me Anne Pynn?"

"Marry you Finn? What to say, what to say?"

"Say yes!"

The recent, ominous discovery loomed like the menacing mask

of a mummer, standing between the two us preventing me from accepting his proposal.

"Let me go to Boston and find my father. When I get back I will give you my answer."

"I will take that as a promise, a promise you must keep and seal with a kiss."

Then Finn took me in his arms and kissed me with all the pent up passion that he had been holding back.

His hands rustled my clothes, reaching through fabric.

"We must wait." I insisted, declining his physical advances.

Did we wait?

I pause in my manuscript, my almost autobiography. I gaze again across the slope of terraced lawns bewitched by the lithe form sitting barefoot on the ground. An enchanting little fairy stares up at the wispy clouds whose imaginative shapes fill the sky.

It is not an apparition.

It is Belle, my princess, my auburn haired, miracle child. Seemingly born without oddities. No outward signs of the unusual. She has two arms, two legs, two hands and two feet. When she was born, I frantically examined her tiny body counting ten fingers, ten toes. She sees, she hears, she claps her hands in childish glee. Every single day, I thank the creator for the perfect vision of her, the faultless sound of her. Sometimes when I see her through the window like this, it is akin to staring into a crystal ball. I am at once joyous for her life and fearful for her being. About the internal workings of her mind, I cannot be absolutely sure. She is curious and undecidedly clever. She has a convincing intuitiveness, good judgement and a quick wit. I sometimes observe a fleeting moment of wisdom beyond her years. Then I ask myself the eternal questions.

Did she inherit any of Bridie's special powers?

Is there somewhere deep within her seat of consciousness, abilities passed down from my mother?

And what of myself?

Is there a part of me enclosed within her tiny frame? Perhaps my animated spirit, my will to face a challenge head on, has been sewn onto that youthful skeleton. I want her to be all three of us: Bridie, my mother and me. And yet, I want her to be just simply Belle. She is my daughter, but she also belongs to Finn. Prostrate at her birth, while a detached placenta left me drowning in viscous red blood, I gave her to him. Finn promised to cherish her all the days of his life. I surfaced gasping for life's precious air from the depths of that crimson pool. I healed, but there will never be another child. Perhaps this is just as well-----------------

The patients from Pynn Place and Lace House ask, "What is your name little girl?"

And she replies, "Belle, from umbelliferae."

They raise their eyebrows with a questioning expression.

"You know, the flower." And as an afterthought she adds, "and my mother didn't die."

Is there a message in that simple statement?

When she is older, I will give my daughter this book. She will read about our family, she will discover the truth, not the raw cutting truth but the truth wrapped in the cushion of a mother's love. There now, out of the corner of my eye, I see Finn coming across the lawn to greet his mini minx as he calls her. He pauses to speak with the old man, putting an arm about his crooked back, pointing at a few of the beautiful blooms of pink and purple lupine and the immaculate white of the daucus carota that have been tenderly cultivated. He reaches for Belle as she teasingly chases in circles about his legs. The two, father and daughter will go together, hand in hand to visit the wards, listening to and talking with the inmates of Pynn Place. I consider the medicines, ponder the doctor's prescriptions, and contemplate the respite care and the solitary confinement out here at the Lake. Then, I reflect upon Belle. I truly believe that it is the human touch of this happy-go-lucky lass, that offers a cure for all these ailments, whether physical, emotional or spiritual. Yes, I perceive without hesitation a suggestion of Bridie's presence in the stroke of an arm, the touch of a hand, the brush of a cheek. I recognize as well, the strong branch of a tree reaching out from the past to support the weight of a little girl who dares to climb and sit in its crux.

At Lace House, the girls look forward to Belle's breezy entrance. Her daily arrival is an important event. She does not judge them. Her innocence attracts them. Soon they each will have a child of their own. They must decide what strength there is in the branches of their own trees. They must decide to fold their arms and hold their child close, or open their arms and let it go. In some strange way having Belle around makes the choice for them easier.

Deer Inn, our third and final institution. Finn and I agonized over this facility. It was never our intention to accommodate an orphanage. But the girls, they came and they left. The babies they came and most often, they didn't leave. Out of necessity grew Deer Inn. Finn came up with the name after the original Saint Brigid's Kildeer Place in Ireland, after Deer Hospital in Boston and after Oscar Sweetapple, his father. You have to understand that the name Oscar means deer. All the symbolic interpretations captivated my imagination. Finn and I were clever and inventive, we were, we were.

Belle loves the babies. I try to tell her she shouldn't get attached because many of them will be adopted. She doesn't listen. She rocks them, coos to them and mothers them with maturity beyond her years. A few have stayed because of a mental or physical incapacity, they are not chosen. They play with Belle, go to school with her, they are like the brothers and sisters that she will never have.

All the buildings are frame, one blue, one white and one rust.

The blue one is Pynn Place. The blue wrapped around it like a mother's robe, protecting and loving. The white one is Lace Place, needing no explanation. The rust one is Deer Inn, shod in camouflaged crimson, with the vagueness and anonymity of the blood mystery.

Through the window, the seasons like the patients come and go. Regardless of the season, the weather is almost always cold and I must bundle up in a warm sweater and sip hot tea. On this particular day I am doing more reminiscing that writing. In the bottom of the hot cup, which warms my freezing fingers, I can see a sediment of leaves and my thoughts flit back to Henrietta's readings. As she predicted, there has been sadness in my life. I have found love. I have created love, abundant love. But money and wealth elude me. Henrietta said, "You will be rich some day." Perhaps I misinterpreted her meaning, for I am rich with family, friends and Finn. Finn who has kept his promise and stayed for as long as I've needed him. Although he didn't save a King's land, like his namesake he kept the land his grandfather gave him. Like his namesake he didn't marry the King's daughter. I turned down his proposal. This is what I told him.

"Once upon a time there was an island called Land of White Lace. The King who ruled the island had only one descendent, a handsome white haired youth who was his grandson. When the lad grew to be a man, the King sent a message across White Lace searching for a wife for the young prince. The people who lived on the island all had white hair; they adored the King and his grandson. One white wolf was the only animal that existed. It circled about the island protecting the people. There was only one bird that lived there. It was a white swan. The people watched over the swan, they fed it and protected it. The big white bird swam about the waters surrounding the island shielding the mermaid who lived beneath the sea. The mermaid had long white hair.

One day the mermaid rose up from the deep with a baby in her arms. It was a baby girl with flaming red hair. She placed the baby on the back of the swan where the wee lassie grew into a beautiful young maiden. The swan swam ashore and left the girl at the feet of the wolf. The wolf picked her up and carried her on his back all the way to the King. The Prince who was standing by the castle door fell instantly in love. The King stared at the woman in disbelief. "She has red hair. This will never do. My grandson cannot marry anyone who does not have white hair, the white hair of our people. If he does, a terrible tragedy, the devils plague will descend upon the island."

Whereupon the Prince fell to his knees begging his grandfather to let the girl remain. Grabbing at the royal robes, the Prince beseeched his grandfather to lift the curse of the white hair and to give his blessing on a union between himself and the bewitchingly beautiful red haired maiden.

"She is welcome to stay in the Land of White Lace but a royal decree is passed stating that you two shall never wed. These are my final words on the subject." Responded the grandfather. So the young girl stayed and lived beside the Prince and loved him for the rest of her life.

Finn studied me when I had finished. A far away look came into his eyes and he seemed to understand.

If I was truly an artist and could paint, if I had inherited my mother's talent, I would capture the charm of the Newfoundland seasons forever on canvas. Instead, I try to establish a mental image on paper with the written word. In the summer, roses creep up the latticework of trellises on the south walls of the buildings. Blush pink; crimson red and creamy white roses climb the grate in abundance. Curtain corners escape from open windows while summer's cacophony filters in through these same openings; birds chirping, grasshoppers buzzing and frogs croaking Through the casement I hear another sound, a familiar creek and realize it is the gentle motion of the runners of the red, blue, yellow and green rocking chairs rubbing against the wide veranda floors. The empty chairs lined up straight backed like sentinels sway freely. Belle is often the culprit of this rocking as she jumps from chair to chair, setting them in action with a tap of her foot or a push of her hand or the pumping of her dimpled legs. The rapid see saw motion as they rock back and forth manufactures a kaleidoscope of colour. I've been told that the soft lulling to and fro that provides a peaceful pastime is also a form of healing. The ghosts of Pynn Place sit in those chairs, rocking, rocking and watching over all who reside within its walls.

A homemade swing hangs from an ancient willow, where carved in the bark are mine and Finn's initials. I don't ever recall putting them there but someone must have. A melee of wildflowers speckles the ankle deep grass beneath the wooden seat. If one swings high up in the air and looks leeward there is a glimpse to be had of shimmering Lady Lake.

Finn enjoys recounting to me that it was during summertime hundreds of years ago that an exceedingly beautiful maiden, wearing a crown of red gold on her head and riding a snow-white steed, met the legendary Irish Oisin Cumhal on the sparkling shores of Loch Lena. She called out to Oisin, "I have come on a long journey and at last I have found you. Will you come with me to the Land of Youth?" Oisin, having fallen under the woman's spell agreed to give up all his earthy ties and go as her lover. The two journeyed on the white mount over many oceans and through many forest glades down through time. Down through time to the shores of a fishing village in Newfoundland, where another Oisin was coerced by another maiden.

Summer is slow to come and quick to go. .

Autumn brings it's own pleasure. And it's own reminders of the past. It was in the fall that I began my first job at the sister's shop. The sisters have long since both passed away. The shop is no longer a millinery but has been transformed into a book store. After I returned from Boston, I worked at P & P's until Belle was born. Both Phoebe and Prudence thought that since I was with child, it was imperative that Finn and I be married. They even created a special bonnet for my wedding day. Of course a marriage was not to be and the bonnet not to be worn. Like Bridie, I had my child; unlike her I never exiled the father. After recounting to Finn the fable Land of White Lace, he accepted his role as a guardian. As the custodial head of Pynn Place he is as much a part of the facility as I am. He is my official sentinel watching over me and keeping me safe. He is Belle's protector, her guardian angel and as much a part of her life as I am. I kept the wedding bonnet, stored it away in the unlikelihood that someone, someday would wear it. Once when my mother was painting an autumn landscape she told me that like her, Jack Frost dipped his paintbrush into pots of golds and rusts, touching the leaf tips with the russet shades of the season. My mother had an uncanny attachment to trees in their various stages of dress and undress. She would find a half dead tree, or one denuded of its foliage and with her artist's skill, transform it, making the lifeless branches come alive. With a flick of her wrist forlorn twigs acquired new and bedazzling attire. Gnarled trunks developed smiling faces. Burrowed stumps became homes for forest creatures. I often wondered how my mother could so easily make a sad tree happy and yet she was unable to nourish happiness within herself, to take away her own sadness.

Bridie died when fall was in its full regalia and for that reason alone it is a marked season.

What of winter? Winter camouflages the earth's secrets. It is a time to sit close to the fireside, a time for the telling of tales and myths. I once asked my mother how she got her name. Charlotte said she was named after the Druscilla butterfly whose white wings looked like her white hair. My mother's version of the story was much more exciting.

> *"Before I was born, Blind John had an Irish buddy who use to come around and help with chores. He would shout at his buddy, "Hey Irish, chop wood for the fire. Hey Irish, fill up the water bucket. Hey Irish, take my rifle and find us a meal. Hey Irish, take my pole and land us a fish." When the chores were finished, the two would sit at the back door smoking their pipes, telling jokes. They had the comical rapport of best friends. Blind John hadn't any money with which to pay Irish so he whittled him a gift, a wooden butterfly. Irish named it his Druscilla. Irish died of consumption and Blind John wanted to honour his buddy so he named me after his Druscilla."*

I was born in winter in the midst of a blizzard. Bridie said the snowdrifts were waist deep and piled high, right up to the window ledges. There were icicles hanging from the eaves long enough to touch the ground. It was so cold that the front door of the house was frozen shut. Out in the barn the farm animals huddled together in one area of the stable, collectively trying to create some heat. For days the whole village was frozen. Nothing moved. It was like a picture my mother might have painted, a winter scene in arrested animation.

Winter is mine. Winter is white. White clouds, white snow, white ice, white Christmas, white hair, white linen, and the white heat of passion. If anyone ever asked me to choose a colour that most represents Finn, it would be white. My white is translucent; his white is solid, packed hard like winter ice.

Spring is for Brigid. It is Imbolc. Beginning February first, a harsh, bitter month but through the still frosted glass windows of my room, I see the magic wand in Old Woman Winter's hand, as she waves it aloft bringing the earth to life. Birds begin their nest building, lambs are born and the ewe's milk flows. Fishermen impatiently await the signs that they can launch their boats after the long winter's solstice. Children break forth, out into a world where a new sun begins to turn everything from white to green.

Spring is a time for romance. Where is my romance? There it is, there lined up on the mantel. My glass menagerie; a puffin, wolf, swan, mermaid, a filigree flower, ornaments, so many ornaments trail there way across the shelf; all tokens betelling the story of Finn's adoration. There, nestled amongst them is the encased photo. The photo of my father, which had waited so long to finally be framed.

CHAPTER 16

1919

DELILAH

Harlot heroine
sent coins
to
feed us
clothe us
shelter us.
Golden coins
like golden people
appear
to
disappear.

In the end Finn came with me to St. John's. I had come to the point where I couldn't bear to be apart from him but at the same time I felt so guilty with deception, that neither could I face him. He pleaded to be allowed to accompany me as far as Delilah's and since my conscience was bothering me, I agreed. Weeks earlier when I had written to Delilah describing the circumstances of my trip, asking if I might stay with her for a few days, I had mentioned that a young gentleman might be accompanying me. A return letter was delivered promptly expressing her pleasure at my impending arrival.

"Naturally you are most welcome in my home. Sam and I look forward to seeing you and perhaps your young friend. We will be glad to meet you at the station."

On the day before our departure Finn and I went to tell his grandfather. I had been reluctant to pay Sweetie Pie a visit ever since the 'day of discovery' but I had to pretend nonchalance and not show any hesitation whilst in his presence, for Finn's sake. Oisin, the wonderful gentleman that he was, gave me his blessing and said, "I will pray that you have a safe journey and that you find your father. Then come back to us dear Anne, please come back to us." He didn't appear to give a second thought to Finn and I travelling in each other's company, for which I was relieved. Nor did he flinch at the mention of my search for my father.

We went together to P & P's and I explained the entire situation, apologizing for leaving them without a clerk. The dear ladies were so kind, they wished me good luck and told me that when I came back if I still wanted to work, my job would be waiting for me, just a few hours a week, just like it had always been. They made me think about Finn's plans for Pynn Place and about my promise to give him an answer to his marriage proposal. I started to feel apprehensive, to get cold feet as the expression goes, thinking perhaps it would be best to just let life go on as it had been. Living with Aunt Charlotte. Selling hats. No man in my life. No demands on my emotions. No travelling. No predictions of marriage. My mind was miles away, perplexed at the thoughts of everything I was about to undertake and the many decisions I would soon have to make; when Phoebe tapped me lightly on the shoulder and handed me a mauve silk bonnet with the widest of ribbons to tie under my chin.

"For your trip, my dear, for your trip." Said Prudence

"How can I thank you, it is just the right colour to compliment my hair."

"Just come back my dear, come back."

Everyone was concerned for my well-being, concerned for my return, afraid that I too would vanish into the Newfoundland mist as my father had done before me. Everyone wanted me to come safely back home.

Next we confronted Charlotte. She seemed ambivalent. No galling speech when Finn and I announced our exodus for the following day. As soon as Finn went home to make his last preparations for the trip, it was then that she accosted me.

"You are walking into waters that are too deep for you, you will surely drown."

"Auntie, what are you talking about, drowning? I am going in search of my father. I must do this. You know I must."

Taking my hand in hers, she tried to convince me not to make the trip.

"Please my dearest, do not go. Stay here with me, where you are safe and happy."

"No Auntie, I have made my decision." I insisted. "I will not be happy until I find my father."

"I wish there was something I could say that would sway you, stop you. When we go in search of the past, things are revealed to us that we might not like or might not want to accept. I hope and pray that this does not happen to you."

Thinking that she might be trying to warn me that Shadrach could be dead, I told her, "Try not to worry, if I do not find him, or if he is dead then I will have at least tried my very best to give some kind of conclusion to His life and I will be at journey's end for that part of My life. I will be able to get on with the next chapter. You might as well know if you haven't already guessed, that I am in love with Finn. He has asked me to marry him and I have promised to give him an answer when I return from Boston. The truth is I cannot give him an answer until I find my father. Can you not understand how important this is to me?"

"As much as you may not realize it, in my own way I have loved and cared for you like a daughter. I often feel what you feel, hurt when you hurt, I am just not very good at expressing my sentiments. If you must go, be cautious. If you find your father, I hope that you will not be saddened or disillusioned. No matter what happens, no matter where your search leads you, please Anne, know that you can always, always come home."

I hugged her then, feeling her frail little body in my arms. "I am not abandoning you, I will come home." I promised.

I left her then and went to my room to finish packing for the trip. After arranging the last few things into my suitcase, I placed the hat pin, my father's photo and the packet of my father's letters on the top of my neatly folded garments. I hadn't read the letters yet. I planned to do so on the steamship as I sailed to Boston. They were the last of the items in the box. I knew I was avoiding them because subconsciously I didn't want an end to come to the contents. I sensed a conclusion closing in on me. Somehow it would seem so final to read the letters. They were the only remaining untouched connection with my mother and father. I closed the suitcase lid and pushed in the latch on the lock, which I turned with a tiny key, then hung it on a chain around my neck for safekeeping. I laid down on the bed, staring up at the ceiling, thinking about what Charlotte had said. I was baffled. For the past few weeks she had been so subdued to the point that I thought her health might have been failing. Now her reaction to my trip was so different, so out of character. her advice, her last words, so mysterious. Was she hiding something from me? It seemed she was predicting something grim, foretelling an upsetting future, forewarning me of disaster. I tried to shake off the robe of adversity that she had thrown over me by reminding myself that she was always in opposition to anything I did. The sun had gone down and the room darkened.

I must have dozed off, for I heard my mother calling me, "Anne, Anne."

Hovering over Haypook rock, the mermaid beckoned; her long white hair trailing down her back, her curls tossed out into the foam of the surf. I walked across the water where a path opened up for me. Closer, closer to the rock where the half woman, half fish waited for me. Then, with an arch of her great and wondrous tail she dove deep into the waters of the harbour. Her tail flashed, I followed. The path began to sink, submerging first my feet, my ankles, then knees and finally I was floating, swimming, moving closer, closer. I reached the rock and climbed up its slippery surface. I skimmed the horizon. But she was gone – vanished, leaving only a mirror on the rock beside my tail. When I cast my eye into the looking glass, my hair burst into flames; so I too plunged downward in an effort to extinguish the burning halo about my head. Fathoms below my undulating tail took me deeper into the sea world, chasing, searching after the unknown.

Above me the flames burnt on, igniting a circle around the rock.

When I awoke, I was drained from the dream and frightened. I looked down at my feet. Definitely they were there, not a fin but two feet. I breathed in and out, in and out in relief. I did not sleep for the rest of the night.

We took an early morning train. We had seats in the Pullman, which could be turned into a sleeper. After making ourselves comfortable, I told Finn about the dream.

"Its best to examine a dream, to try and make sense of it." He urged.

His knowledge never ceased to amaze me. He recounted the story of the Goddess Brigid and the mermaid.

"The mediaeval Brigid frequently travelled in disguise. Sometimes she presented herself as the ancient sea goddess Marian. Marian was also called the Merrymaid, the name from which came mermaid. Brigid the sea goddess always carried a mirror in her hand. This was a mystery but probably stood for 'know thyself.' I think your dream was a good omen. Your mother was trying to commune with you, to let you know that she approves of your search to find your father and ultimately to know yourself better. I remember the old fable when the Goddess Brigid was born at sunrise; a tower of bright flame burst from her forehead that reached from earth up to heaven. Of course Bridie is the liaison between you, the mermaid in your dream and your father. I find it fascinating how she appears in so many different ways: in your subconscious, in bottled messages and in sleeping reveries. You only have to look at the picture your mother painted when you were born to see yet again the connection between birth, flames and the red hair in your family."

Finn's explanation of the dream eased my mind. Lack of sleep from the night before left me yawning and I leaned my head against his shoulder. The click clack of the engine's wheels as they travelled over the tracks hypnotized me and I nodded off for a short spell, undisturbed by my ancestors. The remainder of the time, we watched the landscape flying by. Having never travelled beyond the limits of the town, I quite enjoyed the scenery as the locomotive chugged its way along 'the people's road', journeying slowly up steep hills and across the flats. The porter who had stacked my luggage in a rack above our heads came through the coach and announced that the noon meal was being served in the dining car. My balance was askew as I walked in the narrow aisle while the train curved around bends and descended a long grade. I had to grip Finn's arm to stay upright. Like the long arm of Harbour Grace, Finn's arm felt strong and safe. Passing from one carriage to the next meant crossing a metal trestle that I was convinced was quite dangerous.

I made the mistake of looking down at my feet where I could see gravel, grass and railway ties flashing beneath the iron grid. The motion had a dizzying affect and I had to tell myself to keep going so as not to swoon. A current of wind that passed through the open space between the cars made forward progress even more difficult as it tended to suck one backwards.

Finally, with Finn's guidance, we made it without incident and I sank down in the plush, scarlet, velvet seats that matched the curtains in the windows. White linen cloths and napkins adorned the tables and our meal was served on china of the finest quality. I was so impressed with everything, from the service to the impeccable menu. The food was delicious. I had ribs of beef, so tender that each bite just melted in my mouth. Roasted potatoes and spears of asparagus shared my plate with the meat. For dessert, there was the tartest of lemon pies with a meringue that had to be at least three inches high. I felt like a princess, being waited upon by all my entourage of servants. After sipping a last cup of coffee we retired to the sleeper. I wondered if this would present a problem; if there would be an intimacy over sharing the room, a proximity created that I was ill prepared for. But Finn put pillows on the floor and reclined there for a nap. I awoke to the shrill of a long sharp whistle hailing our arrival at the Reid depot in St. John's. The room was stuffy, my mouth dry my dress dishevelled, my jacket creased and my hair in disarray. Using a little washbasin in the tiniest of closets, I splashed some cold water on my face and tried to freshen up as best I could for our meeting with Delilah. She was on the platform waiting to greet us, standing beneath the station's pillared portico, dressed in a flamboyant red suit, waving a matching red scarf.

A monument to the railway system, the terminal in St. John's was one of the few buildings in the city not constructed of wood. Stone from the Reid family quarries had been used in the assembly of the prominent structure located at the end of Water Street. The road itself leading up to the grand entrance had been paved with Reid granite blocks. Delilah's stiletto heels click clacked over the stones as she rushed forward in a gushing greeting, a waft of her expensive perfume enveloping us. Crushing me in her arms and hugging me, she explained the absence of her husband. Apparently Uncle Sam was unable to accompany her for our arrival, as he had important business to attend to in the heart of the city. I was just as glad as I was certain that my appearance would not have made a very good impression on him. Compared to my aunt, I looked rather like the beggar woman standing by the station door, holding out a basket, in hopes that a few of the arriving passengers might slip a coin or two her way. Delilah promptly obliged the pleading look on the woman's face.

"There but for the grace of the good lord, go I." She announced. "The train system is a mystery to me. How those black engines can pull all those cars laden down with people and luggage through the remotest area confounds me. How they can bring the rest of Newfoundland right to our doorstep here in St. John's with seemingly the slightest effort is perplexing. And look that mighty, black beast of a machine brought you here all the way from Harbour Grace."

"Aunt Delilah, this is Finn Sweetapple, my friend whom I mentioned to you in my letter."

She took a long drawn out look, giving him a good stare in the eyes, surveying him from head to foot.

"More than a friend is my guess." Delilah had never donned the airs of the rich. She was unrefined in speech and manner. Brigid said she had always been a good judge of character.

"I'm pleased, very pleased to make your how do. Call me Dee." She requested. "Everyone here knows me by that name. Come, I've hired a driver to take us home."

I half expected to see a horse drawn carriage but it was an automobile that she bundled us into.

"This is a city of intrigue. It is like me, it has two faces." Declared Delilah. "There are many ugly back lanes and haunting dark paths giving it a forlorn look, especially in inclement weather. But, when the sun shines it is breathtakingly beautiful offering an unblemished countenance. Beneath the cake powder, mascara and make up I am haggard and worn but on the surface my wrinkles are artificially smoothed and despite my age I still have a dashing smile."

Pointing out a few landmarks as we made our way through the winding streets, Dee drew attention to St. John's Cathedral. Animatedly describing its historical background, she told us that the Church was a testament to the faith and fortitude of the Irish Catholic population in conjunction with the determination of many Protestants. The two groups had laboured long hours and sixteen years to see the church erected. It was a mixture of the old and new world. Local sandstone had been combined with limestone from Galway and granite from Dublin to shape the main building. Two tall towers, containing a clock and Irish bells, flanked the main section. The bells could be heard peeling out over the entire city. An archway leading into the grounds had been built in roman style with a statue of St. John the Baptist mounted atop the centre of the three arches.

After almost colliding with a streetcar, we pulled onto Circular Road where several prominent citizens lived including Delilah and Sam. Their three-story, wood, frame home faced toward the harbour guarded by two hills, Southside and Signal Hill. Dee displayed even more pride in the city as she told us that it was from Cabot Tower on Signal Hill that the first transatlantic wireless message was received all the way from England.

The wood in the entranceway of the elegant house was polished and gleaming. The marble tiles scrubbed so clean and shining that you could almost see your reflection staring back up at you from the floor. The scent of massive bouquets of spring flowers, lily of the valley and lilac spilled from the parlour. Auntie Dee escorted us up the winding staircase to our separate rooms. Mine was festooned in white; white walls, white rugs, white vanity with white jug and bowl. A giant four-poster bed stood at the room's equator decorated with a chenille spread and candlewick canopy. At the foot of the bed over the blanket rail was a shawl. I fingered it gently. Watching me intently, Delilah asked, "Do you recognize the handiwork? Of course it is Brigid's. She presented it to me as a wedding gift. I adore it."

Dee had an affected way of talking, twirling a curl about her forefinger, then flicking it back at the end of a sentence.

"You can make yourself comfortable in this boudoir, while I deliver Finn down the hall."

A door to one side led to another room, I opened it to take a peek. And there stood a burnished white tub. A bathtub with running water – unheard of! As Bridie had alleged, her little sister had married well.

We toured the remainder of the house. Finn was spellbound with the library, its stacks of books lining the walls from floor to ceiling. Shakespeare, Wordsworth and many other renowned authors, too numerous to mention. The tang of the leather jackets as inviting as the words on the pages within.

"What a collection, wherever did they all come from?" he asked.

"Sam studied at Oxford and when he immigrated from England, he brought them all here to dear Newfoundland. We are most fortunate, don't you think? Go ahead and choose one to take with you back to Harbour Grace, consider it as a little token of my gratitude for you having delivered Anne safely to my doorstep."

I was enthralled with the chandelier in the dining hall. Its twinkling crystals cast dancing shadows on the flocked papered walls. The creamy satin draperies, which embellished the bow windows, dripped of prosperity and the brocade cushions on the window seats spoke softly of wealth. This was not a house – this was a castle. Next we strolled in the well-manicured gardens, Dee pointing out an extensive variety of shrubs and plants. The walkway ambled past fountains, statues and a birdbath. There was even a wishing well. Finn tugged at my arm suggesting a fancy, "Let's make a wish. A wish that we will be together forever."

Then he tossed a coin over the stone wall into the long, dark tunnel. Seconds later we heard the echo of its splash as it hit the water many feet below. Was the wish shattered? Would the truth be told in the resulting ripples it created or resounding sound emanating up the well? I turned my attention back to the glorious garden. I couldn't believe that anyone could have all these wonderfully unique ornaments in their back yard. When the tour was over, we had what Delilah called high tea in the drawing room. There were dainty, triangular sandwiches with sliced cucumber and the thickest of cream cheese, hot sausage rolls and pickled eggs. Neither Finn nor I realized how hungry we were.

"I hope my dearest niece that you will not be offended that I took the liberty of going to the steamship office and purchasing your tickets for Boston. Consider this a little gift from your Uncle and I."

"No, no I must reimburse you. It is very kind but I have saved money from my job in the millinery and Finn has also contributed."

"Nonsense, you will accept our gift, it is naught and there will be absolutely no more discussion on the matter. Now the ship leaves port the day after tomorrow, quite, quite early in the morning, so you must try to get good a nights sleep, both tonight and tomorrow. Travelling is always exhausting and I find there is no better way to relax one's mind and body than by having a good old-fashioned soak in the tub. Please both of you, avail yourself of these amenities, you will find all the toiletries you require in the bathrooms. Now if you'll excuse me, I am not getting any younger and I need my beauty rest so that when Sam comes home I can still make an impression upon him. Good night my dears and pleasant dreams."

Having said all of this, Delilah went off with a sweep of her majestic maroon dressing gown, leaving Finn and I to fend for ourselves.

"I will return home on tomorrow morning's train." Finn announced.

"You have your tickets and I can clearly see you will be well attended to by your Aunt. My leave taking will provide the opportunity for the two of you to visit unimpeded by my presence. I'm sure there are many things you would like to discuss about your family and I must get back to Grandfather and Pynn Place. Now it's to bed with you. The next few weeks will be very demanding, so you must get plenty of rest as Delilah suggested. Good night, my lovely and charming Anne." He kissed me then, lightly on the cheek. Something hot ran through my veins.

In my room surrounded by white, I felt pleasantly exhausted. But, I decided not to miss the chance to take a bath in the gleaming ivory porcelain tub. It was all peculiar, foreign to me. There was a rubber plug attached to a silver chain, which needed to be inserted into the drain to prevent the water from running down the pipes. Two sparkling taps marked with an H and C fed water rapidly cascading out of something called a faucet. Back home we still hand pumped water into big pots and basins. Stripping down, I stepped over the side and lowered myself into the hot sudsy water. I was astonished at this contrivance explicitly invented for the sake of cleansing the body.

For me, pure, unadulterated luxury.

On shelves bordering the enclosure Delilah had arranged bath oils, perfumes and a profusion of creams for the sole purpose of the user having an adventure in relaxation. I loved the silky feel of the hot water against my skin. Strange sensations were erupting in my groin. I closed my eyes and immersed myself even further. I imagined Finn standing above me, looking down at my nakedness. Trailing a hand over my breasts and abdomen, down between my legs. Separating, separating with the kindness of his fingers. He lifted me tenderly out of the steam, carried me quietly and laid me gently upon the Queen Anne's Lace. The flower burst open in full bloom. Finn rolled the pip ever so lightly and it grew. Someone pulled the silver chain and the heat and the white and the water dispersed.

"Will the mother die?" I screamed.

I opened my eyes. I was on the bed enveloped in white. Finn was crouched above me.

In the morning when I awoke, I couldn't move. Alone in the bed I was cold and paralysed with fear. What had we done? What had

I done? Had we joined our bodies in the white heat of passion or had I been dreaming. There was an indentation in the pillow next to mine and in my hand a few stands of white hair. Finn had taken the whiteness of my body and was gone. Gone on the train back to Harbour Grace. Gone. And I was alone in a stained white bed. My mother had been alone when my father left. Alone in a field of white and it had destroyed her. Was Finn like my father? I didn't know. I did know that I was in love with him. Some people say that women are attracted to men who are by nature like their father. After all a girl's first love is suppose to be her father. On the other hand some people suggest that because a girl is like her mother in character, it is that likeness which draws her to a man similar to her father. But I wasn't like my mother. I felt sure that I was more akin to Bridie. My mother and father grew up together; they loved each other from birth. Decidedly it was fate, which brought Finn and I together. The question was – where would fate lead us now?

I could smell the aroma of coffee wafting up the servant's stairs from the scullery. I put on my dressing gown and went to find my Aunt. She and Sam were sitting in the room referred to as the atrium sipping the fragrant brew. Fresh rolls, jams and jellies were on a tray in front of them. A silver pitcher holding thick white cream sat next to a bowl of sugar cubes. There was a pair of miniscule silver tongs with which to pinch and retrieve the sweet white squares. The white cream, the white squares and the pinching hurled me backward to the night before. I swayed and grabbed the back of Sam's chair to steady myself. He was reading the daily edition of the newspaper and Dee having finished giving herself a manicure, was painting her nails. When she had completed her task of vanity she invited me to join her in her personal bureau.

"Here I keep all official papers, letters, documents, wills and correspondence." She informed me, flicking her hair. "I feel important in this room."

Above the mantel was a picture of the nine Pynn children. I asked Delilah to tell me about them.

"Ah yes, I was just a wee one in that picture, barely one year old, sitting there in Bridie's lap. She was my guardian angel and I walked in her shadow. Everyone thought we looked so much alike with our rhapsody of red curls. Seventeen years and seven brothers separated us. The photo was taken just shortly before the death of our parents. My father died in a great ice storm. He was a sealer. His ship was lost at sea when gales of tremendous force blew huge chunks of ice into the harbour. Seven men in total aboard his barque were killed when a main mast came crashing down as the howling winds and blizzard ravaged their boat. My mother was out in the storm, battling the elements along with so many of the other wives, watching and waiting for the return of their loved ones. It was bitterly cold. My mother must have caught a chill. She became dreadfully ill with pneumonia and died just three days after my father. The eight of us were left in Bridie's care, who became our mother at the tender age of seventeen. Our parents had come to Newfoundland or Terre Nova, as they called it, from Ireland when Brigid was a baby. The rest of us were born in the new land. From the beginning Bridie was an unusual child. She had powers that no one really wanted to discuss. If the goats wouldn't milk, she would go to them, chattering softly and pat them. Next day their teats would fill the pails. If crops seemed meagre, she would water them and they flourished. One time, I was told, some neighbours came to our farm to visit. Their boy collapsed on the kitchen floor, frothing at the mouth his arms and legs shaking wildly. Bridie held his head in her hands and soon he returned to normal. There are many episodes that I could tell you about, but it doesn't really matter. Bridie was Bridie and we all knew what she was capable of and rather than questioning or discussing it, we accepted it.

My oldest brother Joseph was born the year the family arrived. He grew to be a strong, swarthy man and took to the sea just like his father. He married a local girl but they never had any children and this saddened Joseph. In this picture you can see he was fatherly with his arm around both Bridie and Charles who was the brother next in line. Charles never had the physical strength of Joseph but he was the most musical of us all. He mastered just about any instrument put in front of him. He liked his screech too. He and his wife Mary bought a tavern in Twillingate. She ran the saloon and he played the old piano that came with the place. They had one son Charles junior; it was rumoured that he was really the child of the frisky bar maid, but Charles never openly admitted to the hearsay and Mary raised the boy as though he was her own flesh and blood. My brother Henry was the only one of the clan who had a temper to go with the red hair. As an infant he apparently used to bang his head against the wall. His feisty nature managed to manoeuvre him into brawls and fist fights. Bridie always had to rescue him from these dilemmas and then he would turn on her, venting his anger even more. But he was a big help to her just the same, fetching water from the well, chopping wood for the stove and constantly mending and repairing broken down fences. He married late in life and after only a year of wedded bliss, his wife died of consumption. Edward, the middle child, was a gambler. He would place a bet on anything; who could down their swill the fastest, which tree would grow the tallest. He used to hang around Cochrane racecourse. One day, one of the trainers boosted him up onto the back of a black mare, gave her a smack on the rump and off she trotted at full tilt with Eddie hanging on for his life. From that day on he was hooked. Hired as a groom, he wagered all his earnings and was as poor as poor can be. Finally he got a hot tip, kept tripling his winnings, really struck it rich and then moved south to America. As far as I know he's still there, speculating and taking risks. Our little fellow Philip, was called by the sea, just like Joseph. He trailed after his older idol incessantly. When Joseph went to St. Shott on the south shore with a fishing fleet, Philip pestered him until he agreed to take him along. That was back in 1864 when Philip was thirteen. Disaster struck when a great tidal wave rolled in covering the streets and meadows of Shott with tons of water. Many of the villagers lost their homes and businesses, we lost are beloved Philip. He was just swept out to sea. Frances, the frailest son, had a speech impediment. He was born with a split lip and didn't have a roof to his mouth. Nowadays his anomaly is called a cleft palate. Our mother said he was impossible to feed as everything regurgitated out his nose. Bridie hovered over him, spending hours spooning mush into his misshapen orifice and he survived. He eventually married a girl named Lucy who was cross-eyed and had one leg shorter than the other. Frances told her that two freaks of nature were better than one. They moved here to St. John's and raised a family. John our youngest brother accidentally hung himself playing in the barn. He tied a rope about his waist and jumped from the hayloft. Somehow the noose slipped up around his neck and he was strangled. It was a very sad day."

"No one ever told me these stories before, not Bridie, nor my mother. I am grateful to you for relinquishing these important fragments of our family history. Please, tell me more, tell me about yourself."

"For sure, I was the rebel. When I was just about the age that you are now, I packed my bags, left home, left Harbour Grace. Nothing was happening there, I wanted to have fun, party, experience life. I didn't want to end up single, like Bridie, without a man without excitement, or so I thought. I stole some money out of Bridie's jar and made my way here to St. John's but it wasn't quite as easy as I had anticipated. I had very little knowledge of what goes on in the outside world. I guess you could say I was naïve. Once in the big city I rented a room. It turned out to be in a house of ill repute. You understand what that is?"

I nodded not wanting to interrupt her chronicle.

"The madam who ran The Manor for that's what the brothel was called, quickly befriended me and began my formal education into the domain of a paid woman. I started to work for her. You needn't look too surprised as it was a long time ago and life is quite different for me now. I was a prostitute though, just the same. I am not ashamed for that's how I met Sam; he was one of my customers. We fell in love and he rescued me from the disgusting state that I had fallen into. I contracted a disease and though a physician cured me, I was unable to bare children. Sam swore never to enter a whorehouse again. I guess you could consider us lucky for we are quite well off, remember though that material goods are not always what makes one happy."

"I'm glad you shared your past with me. It has made me feel comfortable talking with you. Since Bridie is no longer with us and my own mother has been gone for more than ten years and Charlotte is unapproachable when it comes to shall we say, delicate subjects, I feel compelled to ask your advise on a certain matter. Without going into a great deal of detail, I must first ask if you know who Shadrach's father was? Did you ever inquire or did Bridie tell you in trust who he was?"

"No my dear, I was never privy to that information. You realize that I left home before Bridie became pregnant. Curiosity often got the better of me and when we were in each other's company, which was not too frequently, I would often steer the conversation subtlety around to the details of her son's paternity. But she never divulged a single word, not even a hint."

"Well, as luck would have it, I ascertained from items left to me in Bridie's will, who the man was. I am not at liberty to reveal his identity, but when the facts became known to me, I also learned a startling truth. In sincere confidentiality I tell you that Finn and I share the same grandfather. In other words, my father and Finn's father were half brothers. Not a soul, not a soul other than you have I confided in. Finn and I fell in love before I was made aware of this situation and now I don't know what to do."

"My darling girl, we never know what little surprises life has in store for us. If you and Finn are meant to be together then as Bridie would admonish, "the gods and the spirits will see that it happens.' I firmly believe that. This is not a grave or life threatening circumstance, my advice to you is leave it to the powers that be."

"Thank you Delilah, thank you for sharing your thoughts on this predicament with me."

"Now Anne, I have something to share with you. Did you ever wonder how Charlotte has managed all these years without seeming to have a source of income? How she raised you with little or no funds at her disposal?"

"No, in fact I guess I never speculated on this."

"When Shadrach left your mother twenty years ago, he came here to St. John's, to this very house and sat in this very room with me. He seemed so sad. He told me that he was going to Boston to reclaim some land that he believed rightfully belonged to the Pynn family. He wanted to make sure that his beloved Druscilla would be taken care of while he was fortune hunting. He explained to me that as soon as he found employment and was earning a living he would send money to me for Druscilla. He knew that Sam had a knack for investing and asked that I give the money to him for that express purpose. When a substantial amount accumulated I was to give it to his wife. For thirteen full years money came regularly from a Boston bank. At the end of each month it arrived, without a note, nor letter, just the money. Sam dutifully put it to work and turned a profit. On one occasion there was a very large sum, this time with a short note, which stated "from sale of Pynn property". Shadrach of course had no knowledge of your existence. He had been explicit that the money was to be for Druscilla. He had also been adamant that no one, with the exception of Sam and myself, be informed as to the benefactor. I thought this strange but nonetheless I swore to him that I would not reveal the origin of the funds. Then one month the envelope didn't come. Sam and I were both perturbed. Sam contacted the bank. They had not received anything that month and they were unable to offer a suggestion as to how to contact the gentleman who had been forwarding the bank notes. There was never another delivery, neither to the bank nor to us. While Druscilla lived with Bridie she didn't appear to need all the money, so Sam kept investing, the principal and the profit. Poor, sweet Druscilla died without ever knowing what her husband had done for her. You my pet were orphaned and claimed in the blink of an eye by your Aunt Charlotte. Bridie had no say in the matter, whatsoever. Charlotte declared that you were her responsibility and took you to live with her. Sam and I agreed not to get involved in the dispute between grandmother and aunt, which arose over your guardianship. Both women only wanted what was best for you.

Bridie relented to Charlotte because she was the younger and your grandmother feared that if you were left under her own protection and something happened to her, it would be just too many adjustments for one already so raw with grief. When it was settled that your custody would be in Charlotte's hands, Sam began to send the interest from Shadrach's money to her on a monthly basis. It was understood that these monthly checks were to be used toward your keeping and upbringing. To this day the principal remains intact. So you see, your father reached out his hand from somewhere unknown to take care of you.

CHAPTER 17

1900

THE LETTERS

Messages
of promise.
Passages
of faith,
harassing hope.
Courier
of life
trespassing
on the mind.

Boston was four days and four nights away. Aboard the steamship I had all those incredibly private hours to contemplate the future, a future that might or might not embrace Finn. I had all those quiet hours to imagine the search for my father: a search that might or might not conclude with a joyful reunion. I had all those silent sequestered moments to read my father's letters.

The ship departed shrouded in an early morning mist. A pearly film loomed over the fishing shacks that marked the harbour's boundaries. Ghostly chimeras of freighters and ferries rose and fell in the haze surrounding their moorings. I waved goodbye to Delilah from the railing of the upper deck as she stood on the wharf in a dove grey suit, blowing kisses in my direction. The boat moved stealthily away and Delilah and the land faded into the clouded hoary horizon.

The sea was rough and the same people who had so jauntily gestured their embarkation to friends and relatives a few hours before, now vomited over the side or rolled with nausea in their bunks. Most of the passengers and many of the crew suffered with motion sickness almost the entire trip, as twelve and fifteen-foot swells played havoc with the S.S. Newfoundland's balance. I did not succumb; to the contrary I found the salty air and the rolling rhythm exhilarating. Watching from the deck I was sure I sited some whales and even an iceberg that the ship came dangerously close to hitting.

The woman I shared a cabin with, who called herself Tess, was one of the unfortunate travellers struck down. Becoming so violently ill and forced to wallow in her bed, she was barely able to converse. I did all that I could to comfort her, putting cool compresses on her brow, giving her small chips of ice to suck on and mopping up after her constant disgorging. Even in her dire straits we were able to form the beginnings of a friendship. Slightly older than me, Tess was very petite. In her stocking feet she couldn't have been more than five feet tall. She had straight raven black hair, cut shoulder length, with flat bangs across her forehead. Grey blue eyes stared out from beneath the fringe. I had never seen a hairdo quite like hers. She told me it was the latest rage in the big city salons. This was her second undertaking to Boston. The first had been as a newlywed with her husband. They had made the decision to move to the great state of Massachusetts to be with his elderly parents. Having been there only a few months she had to return to St. John's to tend to her ailing widowed mother. The mother died in her daughter's arms, thankful that she was able to see her first-born one last time. Although Tess's knowledge of Boston was sparse, she did tell me that it was easy to avoid the confusion of traffic, the twists and turns of the cobble stoned pavement by using the ingenious Boston elevated. This she informed me was a rail line, for public transportation built above the city's streets and buildings. She warned me that there were beggars on almost every corner and pick- pockets who could rob you in the wink of an eye.

"It is a city with a split personality, filled with corruption and strife but invitingly crammed with history and human interest." She said.

"Try not to be intimidated, appear to know where you are going and what you are doing. That way there will be less chance of you becoming a victim of pleading hands and prying fingers."

During daylight hours of the trip I stood either at the bow, enthralled by the wind in my hair, or at the stern watching the turbulent path left by the ship as it pushed forward towards its destiny. The lap of waves against the ship's hull almost hypnotized me so that when my eye glimpsed the illusory undefined line of the horizon where sky met sea, the mirage of my mother's Irish chieftain beckoned. One day I followed the summons and accidentally went below, deep into the ship's belly. Mistakenly, I entered the boiler room where grimy faced men in soiled clothes and covered in soot shovelled loads of coal into the furnaces. They sang in lilted accents, booming out tunes of their forbears, making it impossible to distinguish one from the other. In my fantasy they all became chieftains. Possibly one was my father.

"Shadrach, Shadrach." I called out. No one looked up.

I turned and ran crying back to my cabin.

Inside the small compartment, our living quarters for the next four days, I settled for the top bunk, as Tess had chosen the bottom, less dangerous one. There was a little round porthole right beside my head that I could gaze out and behold the vastness of the ocean. At night the moon was full and so bright that the moonbeams dancing on the water poured in to provide enough light for me to read by. I ventured to open the letters, which were scrawled on splotched paper and hand written by my father. His penmanship was distinctive, the characters small, well defined and formed precisely. I remembered how my Mother recounted to me in her letter that she had taught him the alphabet, had taught him to write. For these letters he had used a quill feather and black ink. To finally expose the contents of his correspondence gave me an eerie, nervous feeling.

April 1899

Dearest Druscilla:

I am writing to tell you that I arrived in the port of St. John's on the schooner Annie Belle this morning, April 1st. In three days time we leave for Boston. I did not know how to tell you face to face, that I was going. I was so afraid that if I looked into your eyes, my own twin eyes would reflect my inner fear and reservation. I was afraid that those eyes would peel out a terrifying reverberation, the resulting echo in my head preventing me from leaving. My mind has not been right since the death of our sweet, sweet Gael. I have been on the brink of insanity. Worthless is the only word that describes how I feel about myself. I needed to get away from the entire depressing situation or I think I would have gone completely mad. I saw Doc Noseworthy and he referred to my condition as a severe depression, a nervous collapse. If going to Boston is a means to calming my frenzied thoughts, regaining some composure and stability of mind, then all will not be lost. In an effort to help cure myself, I am going to try to find the land that once belonged to our family. This hunt will give me purpose and if I am successful I will feel that I have done something worthwhile with my life.

I know that we swore to each other never to be parted. You must forgive me Druscilla for breaking our oath. You must trust me when I tell you that this is for the best. Please take care of yourself and Bridie. I know the one thing you can do to ease the separation is to draw. Draw now, like you have never drawn before, let your feelings spill onto the canvas, let them discharge onto fresh gesso, vacating your mind. This will help you to survive the loneliness that I know will fill your heart, the loneliness already pouring into my own heart.

Do not wait for my letters, for they may not come. Do not wait for me, for I may not come. Begin to make a life for yourself without me whilst I begin to search for peace of mind. I will never stop thinking of you and I will always, always love you.

Shadrach

How deeply my parents had loved each other. How deeply they had reached into each other's minds. It is sad that my father felt compelled to leave his soul mate and his home to regain lucidity, to get back to a healthy state. That separation from my mother had obviously caused him great grief. He must have been torn in two at the thought of leaving her and yet he still left. All their intertwined lives, they had revelled in each others joy, leapt together in ecstasy, soothed each others sorrow and consoled themselves in defeat. What had happened to that strong, unbreakable bond that held them together? Was the birth of my deformed sister the sharp knife that had shorn the indestructible link? Ever since Bridie's funeral and discovering my sister's grave in the cemetery, I have asked myself what it would have been like to have a sister by my side: a sister to grow up with, to share secrets with, to laugh and cry with. If my sister had been born normal and had lived, it is quite possible that my parents and she and I would be living a normal happy family life. Then again if my sister had never been conceived, my parents may never have been married and where would that leave me?

May 1899

Dearest Druscilla:

I have arrived safely in Boston. It took six days. We were warned upon leaving Newfoundland that storms were brewing, the only storms that really occurred were the ones inside my head. I keep asking myself: are my actions pure? My opinion of myself is low, disturbed and divided. On the one hand I feel decent, proper and honourable, yet on the other hand, immoral. Without you, I am lost. Without you, I am only half a person. If I could hold you, whisper to you of my feelings, tell you all that troubles me, then I would be whole again. But there are principles involved.

I remind you of your promise not to write to me.

I am alone and I must find myself.

I know that you are suffering; I can feel it in my heart.

You are alone and you must find yourself.

My only wish is that you do not despise me for leaving you. Oh my wonderful, caring, Druscilla, let me not speak of these trying issues anymore, instead I will tell you a little of my voyage and our arrival.

Our sea passage was without incident. That is to say, the sun shone its blessings on our sails and a constant wind steered us straight on course to our destination. We sailed into the narrows like a ghost in the depth of night. The clouds hung low, visibility was poor but we could hear the distant warning of a fog bell. The captain called the night "pitch black". Afraid of going aground on a treacherous ledge, which he said was close at hand, we anchored off a small island to wait for daybreak and a clear view into the harbour. A few of us who were itching to put our feet on solid ground, launched a small dinghy and rowed to the island, which was perhaps a few hundred feet away. It was a starless sky, with only a thin crescent of a moon but a blinking light created a path on the water's surface. We pulled up on a rocky shore and scampered up to the top of a hill where the lighthouse loomed. The chaps I was with named it "the Bug Light" because it resembled a giant insect on stilts. All around was a profusion of wild raspberries, so we filled ourselves with their sweetness. It reminded me of the times we went berry picking for Bridie, just you and I, hand in hand out into the fields. How happy we were. I hope you are taking care of yourself. I love you Shadrach.

I find it very strange that my father had insisted that my mother not write to him. Why would he so adamantly request that she not respond to his letters? If his intentions were to find the Pynn land, recover his sanity and return to his home, why wouldn't he want correspondence from his beloved wife? Something was peculiar.

September 1899

Dearest Druscilla:

It has been a little while since I wrote to you last but I wanted to wait until I would have something positive to tell you about. I apologize if the long time has distressed you. Here is my news. I have succeeded on two counts. I have found a place to live in the busy congested South End where there are many other transients like myself. My new home is called Arcadia Lodging House. It is five stories high. Can you imagine? It is built entirely of brick and has what the local people call a mansard roof. A spiral iron staircase winds its way up the front of the structure and in the rear, one balcony with another set of steps serves as a fire escape. There is space enough to accommodate 243 people in this one building alone. On my first attempt to acquire a room, I was disappointingly turned away. Feeling completely destitute, I crossed the street and entered a small but busy eatery. My stomach was growling and I realized for the first time that day I hadn't consumed any food for quite some time. A pretty young girl waited on my table; they call it a booth down here. The coquettish wench had a smart white cap on her head and a frilly pinafore tied about her waist. She stood before me flirting, flipping a pad of paper and chewing the end of her pencil while she talked out of the corner of her mouth. I tell you about her, not to make you jealous for you are far, far prettier than she, but it was just nice to have someone perky to talk to and listen to. After satisfying my belly with fried eggs and the thickest of fresh brown bread, I looked out the window and noticed a man weighted down with bags leaving the front entrance of the lodge. I quickly paid for my meal and dashed over the cobblestones and sure enough, a room had been vacated. The cost of a bed varies from 15cents to 25cents a day, depending on which floor the room is on. Mine being the fourth floor is 20cents.

My other success is that I have found employment. Sure enough it is on one of the tugs used to steer or pilot the larger vessels into the harbour. As always I feel closer to home on the water than on the land. My pay is sufficient to cover the rent, buy food and even have a few pennies left over. My other good news is that I have begun the search for the Pynn land. This is going to be a tedious task but I feel in my bones that good fortune in this endeavour is just around the corner.

I miss you Druscilla. I try not to think about our home in Newfoundland and about the life we shared, for it only makes me sad. Sometimes my heart tightens in my chest and the beat quickens. I know it is at these times that you are thinking of me and struggling with our separation. I close my eyes and stand with palms facing outward in an attempt to send you what little strength I have. And selfishly, I admit, to receive your love, to feel your presence within me. Remembering: your palm on my face, your pulse beating slowly, steadily against my cheek, your pulse quickening beneath my hand on your skin, your pulse racing as our bodies touched. Remembering the dancing days that stretched before us as we waltzed as one in the water.

Always be aware that I have not forgotten our special moments in time and I never will. Love Shadrach.

In this letter there are two leads as to my father's whereabouts. The first being the lodging house and the second his employment on the tug. I make a note to follow these leads as they offer very good possibilities for finding him. Again my father does not mention returning to Harbour Grace, instead the letter sounds more like he is settling in and trying to make a home for himself in Boston. Was this what he wanted to do? Was this his intention all along?

December 1899

Dearest Druscilla

It has been a year since our little Gael came into this world and then so quickly left for heaven. Have you put flowers on her grave for me? I work, I eat, I try to sleep. There are villains in my head. Some days, they scream, "Go home Shadrach, go home." Some days they shriek, "Forget, forget." I am tormented by these demons, which race around inside my skull. I cannot forgive myself for loving you, nor for leaving you. I need to know that you are well and somehow surviving this terrible situation that I have forced upon you.

Is Bridie in good health?

Up until now, I have been adamant that we not correspond but I cannot endure the silence any longer.

Write to me Druscilla. Please, please write to me.

I ache with the desire to hear your voice. I hunger for your touch. I dream of dancing with you, one more time.

Your beloved:
Shadrach.

I wonder if my mother did write. I wonder if it was after this letter that she tried to figure out a way to join my father in Boston. According to Delilah, my mother never told my father that she was pregnant for the second time. I wonder why she never told him. She must have been desperately afraid that the child would not be normal. Am I normal?

June 1900

My darling Druscilla.

I have found the land. The land of my forefathers – Pynn land. It was not as difficult to obtain a deed as I had first concluded. There are no words to describe its beauty. There are acres and acres of it. It is actually outside of Boston, near a small community called Winchester. The eastern edge is on a high escarpment overlooking the Atlantic Ocean, it reminds me so much of home. The land is very fertile; the neighbouring farmers have abundant crops. We have orchards Druscilla, pears, peaches, plums, cherries and apples. Many of the fruit trees are in blossom now and what a sight it is. I know you would love to paint this glorious landscape. But what am I saying, you are not here. You will never be here. I think I should sell the land.

Nothing has changed. I still live at the Arcadia where I have made a few friends. I still have employment aboard the tug. I still miss you. There are things I should have told you Druscilla, there are things I definitely should have told you.

Shadrach

I was born by the time my mother received this last letter.

CHAPTER 18

1920

SHADRACH

Gentle giant
burning with desire.
touched by grief.
He fell
from grace.
Muted!
Marked!
Mocked!
Lost to life
To love.

Tess invited me to her home. She was so appreciative of my assistance during her ocean affliction. I was reluctant to accept her generous offer of hospitality; I didn't want to inconvenience either her or her husband in any way. She insisted.

"Really Anne, it is the least I can do after all you have done for me, nursing me throughout our entire voyage."

The idea of staying with someone I knew and not with strangers (even though it was an acquaintance in its infancy) overruled whatever thoughts of disruption my visit would have on their lives. So I welcomed the opportunity. After disembarking and collecting our belongings, David, Tess's husband, met us in the arrivals terminal. He hugged his wife and kissed my hand like a proper gentleman. He had a moustache that twisted up at the ends, a broad smile that caused his upper lip to curl, exposing the whitest teeth that I have ever seen and I must say, rather a roving eye toward the attractive young ladies gathered around on India wharf. This popular jetty was a long stretch of piers and warehouses overflowing with exotic treasures: brass urns, silks, spices, carved curios and tea brought from far away countries like India and China. We walked across Hay Market where loud, boisterous pedestrians bartered for bargains and there we hailed a car. The city was vibrant and alive with activity. We passed Quincy Market where meat and produce wholesalers prepared their goods to be shipped abroad. The smells from buckets of raw fish, barrels of pickles in salt brine and tubs of old cheese wafted in through the car's open windows.

Discovering that both the ladies in his company were hungry, David ordered the driver to pull up and park in front of the Union Oyster House, which held the honour of being the oldest restaurant in town. A white-gloved waiter who stood at attention a few feet from our table, waiting to take our orders, presented the menus on a silver tray. I barely recognized any of the rare items, which were deliciously described. Unfamiliar specialities like frog's legs, pickled pig's feet and turtle soup that I wasn't sure my palate would accept were offered as suggestions for the daily luncheon. I finally selected a fresh green salad, garnished with prawns. After this rather sumptuous meal and a relaxing glass of white wine, which I must admit went straight to my head and turned me quite tiddily, we piled back into the car and carried on toward my hosts' home.

"There on your left is the Old State House, see the one with the unicorns and lions above the front doors." Tess was excited to show me the sights and landmarks of her newly adopted city.

"Look, to your right is Scollay Square, the amusement pivot of the entire community. Here you can encounter vaudeville acts, burlesque, light theatre, here you can experience the exotic nightlife, whatever your heart desires, it all can be found here in this hub of entertainment. We will have to bring you one evening for some social diversion."

Suddenly the car came to an abrupt halt, almost catapulting the three of us forward off our seats. Bright orange barricades prevented us from venturing any further. Policemen were holding back the crowds of people who lined the streets for several blocks, in fact as far as the eye could see.

"What seems to be the problem?" David asked of the driver. "I do hope that someone hasn't met with an accident."

"I apologize profusely for the delay but unfortunately it can't be avoided. Today is the running of the Boston Marathon. Many athletes come from all over the United States and other countries to contest this prestigious event which had its beginning in 1897. People are prepared to indulge themselves this year because it is the first major race since America won the Great War and it is also the Olympic trials. It is a true mark of athleticism to race the 26 miles on foot. Traffic will probably be stopped here for a half hour, perhaps you would like to get out of the car and watch part of the event?"

At first I was annoyed at the interruption but soon my displeasure turned to enthusiasm as the men went running past, some struggling, some elated, some hunting down victory. Most had faces blackened with grime and patches of perspiration glistened on their muscular bodies. I thought of Finn and how fast he could run over the hills and bluffs of Newfoundland. I imagined him running in a race like this and winning. My hero to the end. Some of the men became dehydrated and had to drop out, while others were beset with cramps, gripping their bellies and falling by the wayside.

"I wonder who will win?" I asked of no one in particular.

"Tomorrow we will obtain a copy of the Boston Herald, the local newspaper and find out who the champion is." replied David.

I admired the forthrightness of this ordinary, honest man and contemplated what it would be like to come to Boston with Finn so that he and David could meet and become friends. Maybe as an alternate plan, I could invite this affectionately warm couple back to Harbour Grace for a visit and repay their hospitality by showing them a splendid time in dear old Newfoundland.

As predicted by our driver, in less than an hour, we were on our way with the thrill of the competition lingering in the air.

The remainder of the ride was uneventful. We arrived at Tess and David's home, where they made me feel most welcome and told me to treat it as my own. It had been a fortnight since I had left my own abode. I missed my room and its comforting walls, which seemed to whisper and lull me to sleep at night. I missed my bed and its thick, downy mattress that swelled under my body and carried me off to dreamland. I missed the familiarity of Pynn Place with its remains of Bridie filling every room, every corner. I missed Finn.

The next morning I set out for Laconia Street and the Arcadia Lodging House.

I envisioned arriving at the door.

Being told my father's room number on the fourth floor.

Climbing the steps one by one.

Knocking on the door.

The door opening.

Me, coming face to face with Shadrach. What would he say? How would he react when I told him that I was his daughter?

The trolley stopped.

"Laconia." The conductor hollered back over his shoulder.

There were tenements all around.

Which one was Shadrach's?

I asked a street worker, "Where is the Arcadia Lodging House?"

He pointed across the road. There was only an empty lot.

"That's an empty lot." I said

"Burnt, burnt to the ground." He said.

"When, when did it burn to the ground?" I asked

"That would be thirteen years ago, in 1907. Big fire. Disastrous fire."

Like the building, I was destroyed. I stood staring at the vacant property, where a few tufts of grass and several weeds had broken through the old, cement foundation, all that remained of what was once my father's home. To have come all this way to learn that the house where my father had lived for seven years was gone, burnt to the ground, I just couldn't believe it. Dispirited and in a quandary, I didn't know what to do next. Did my father survive? Was he a victim of the flames? Did he perish and was he now buried in some pauper's grave, never to be found?

I glanced up and saw a restaurant across the street. Recalling my father writing about this place in one of his letters to my mother, I decided to walk in his steps and go over. I needed to sit down and collect my thoughts. Once inside I ordered a coffee and pastry. When the waitress returned I must have looked a pretty site for she asked if I was unwell. I told her that I had come to visit my father and that I was shocked to find that the building where he had last been reported to be living had gone up in flames.

"I remember that fatal night well." She told me.

"Back then, there was a saloon, shooting gallery, shoe shop and tobacco store on the ground floor. The other five floors were filled with lodgers. It was a disastrous fire. The fiercely burning blaze licked away at the entire wooden contents at a fast and furious pace. There were volumes of smoke, billowing out of the doors and windows. Many of the men overcome by heat and fumes, lost their sense of direction and succumbed to suffocation. I have the newspaper article that was in the Boston Herald; I clipped it out and kept it all these years. Would you like to read it?"

I couldn't speak, so I just nodded my head. She went off to fetch the item.

When she returned, she handed it to me saying: "Take your time, I'll just see to my other customers and then I'll be back."

December 3, 1907 Arcadia Lodging House Fire

By: William Noonan firefighter.

On the gravest of nights at two o'clock in the morning, a fire broke out at the Arcadia Lodge while 159 men lay asleep in their beds. There were rumours that the fire, which started in a closet on the first floor, may have been from spontaneous combustion but may also have been set by a man of unknown identity who had been refused entrance. A young boy, who was sitting in the reading room, discovered the fire. He alerted the desk clerk and night watchman. They sounded the house alarm and immediately started to awake the residents.

The fire raced up the stairs, where it took full possession of the top floor. The first engine to arrive started a line of hose in the front door. The first truck to arrive began rescue operations right away. Some residents jumped out of windows into life nets trying to escape the raging flames. The lodgers were required to lock their belongings and clothing into a box at the foot of their beds. Consequently, most of them were unable to dress before they escaped. Some people managed to make it up onto the mansard roof and from there, were assisted by firefighters to adjoining buildings via wooden planks. All the apparatus used to fight the fire was horse drawn with the exception of one engine, which was a self-propelled steamer. Twenty-eight men died and twenty more were injured.

Was my father one of the twenty- eight, or one of the twenty?

The item concluded with a note from the editor referring to the fate of the victims. Those who were severely burned were transported by ambulance to the Boston General. A few of the very worst cases were taken to Deer Island Hospital.

When she re-appeared, I thanked the waitress for sharing the article with me. I decided that I had struggled with enough surprises for one day and prepared to go back to my home away from home with Tess. Upon reporting my shocking findings and the unfortunate events to David, he suggested visiting the office of vital statistics. He offered his advice.

"You have no way of knowing Anne, whether your father died in the fire or if he was rescued. Perhaps he was one of the lucky ones who came away unharmed. I'm afraid you are going to have to do some detective work of your own in order to eliminate each of the possibilities, until you learn exactly what did happen. Go first and apply for a death certificate. If you are unable to obtain that document, then you can begin to search for information in the records at the hospitals."

Even though my mind was overflowing with foreboding and I desperately feared what I would discover, I agreed that David's plan of attack was a sound one. I went to bed that night having made the necessary arrangements to pursue the search for my father the very next day.

I arrived early the following morning at the library, which was home to the public archives for the entire city. The young clerk who waited on me was friendly and helpful. He listened with an attentive ear as I explained my predicament. After I filled out several, rather ominous forms with as much pertinent information and detail as I could muster, the obliging cleric went off to the appropriate section of the building to search through the cemetery of paper work for

Shadrach Pynn's death certificate. I waited for what seemed like an eternity, sitting on a straight-backed, exceedingly stiff leather chair in a cramped corner of a dirty hallway. The place itself exuded death. I kept thinking and wishing that Finn were with me. I realized that I hadn't communicated with him and that I must write to tell him of everything that had transpired thus far. I waited and I waited. Two or three hours elapsed and I began to worry that I had been forgotten. Just when I was about to get up from my horribly uncomfortable seat and approach someone else at the main desk, the clerk returned. He had a very serious look about his face and I immediately anticipated grave news. Lifting his spectacles up over his eyebrows so that he was able to peer out at me beneath the rims, he reported:

"Madam, I am sorry to inform you, that after a thorough search I was unable to find any record of your father's death."

I was overcome with such a sudden sense of relief that tears gushed down my cheeks and I found myself sobbing uncontrollably, on the strangers shoulder.

"Now, now, this is good news is it not? It most definitely means that your father is alive." The clerk spoke softly while patting me on the back.

He offered me his handkerchief and I dabbed briefly at my eyes, while thanking him for his diligence.

The hours of the morning had already been consumed but I calculated that there was enough time in the afternoon for me to pay a visit to Boston General Hospital. Everyone there was so very charitable. The head matron greeted me with alacrity. She had been a floor nurse at the time of the fire. She recollected all too well some of the men arriving on stretchers and others hobbling in, being supported on either side by orderlies and frantic hospital staff. Most of the victims had skin bubbling with blisters. Some were screaming in pain with their half torn clothes stuck to their oozing burns. Some were delirious, their eyes crazed in shock and their limbs shaking uncontrollably from loss of body fluids. As she described the terrifying scene of that night thirteen years ago, I cringed at the thought of the torture and suffering that everyone had gone through…. the torture that perhaps had been my father's fate.

"Many of the men admitted here," she said, "Were in grave condition and subsequently passed beyond the veil."

I learned that files on all previous patients were stored in cabinets in the basement. She called it the bowels of the earth. I assumed referring to the medical term. Because I was looking for information on someone who was presumed alive, the data was considered privileged. She congenially told me that she would send one of her underlings to investigate, to probe the files for any news of my father. She advised that I return in one day's time. I was weary and longed for this nerve-racking adventure to be over. Upon my return to my temporary home, Tess made me a pot of hot tea, served up with buttered toast and jam. She sat with me as I recounted the fruitless events of the previous few hours.

I did not sleep well that night, tossing, turning and thinking about my father and Finn. In my half waking, half sleeping reverie, the two most important people in my life seemed to melt together and become one. I could not separate them. I recalled how in my dream, the wolf, the swan and the mermaid had appeared to blend together and become one. I thought of how I had discovered that Finn's grandfather and my grandfather had become one. I worried that my dreams too often acted as a mirror for an approaching reality.

I panicked that I was about to expose another becoming of one.

The next morning I made a prompt return to the General Hospital. The matron was just as punctual in receiving me for the second time. It was obvious that she enjoyed her medical prowess.

"There is not a single cell, not a sinew of evidence that Shadrach Pynn was ever a patient here." She informed me.

"Go to Deer Island Hospital, perhaps you will find his files there. Many of the personnel have been there for years and if he was there, might remember him. That institution has a rich human history. Back in the 1600's the undesirables of Boston were banished there. Once it was used to quarantine immigrants. Orphans, paupers and prisoners have all been nurtured, nursed and have recuperated there. Go and see for yourself. Ask questions. Try to obtain some answers or clues as to your father's whereabouts."

Holding her hand out in a farewell gesture she wished me well.

"Good luck, young lady."

An hour later I boarded the little ferry, which took passengers to the Island. With me was my black reticule – my constant companion – containing the photos, the hat pin, the letters, my mother's green ribbon and Bridie's leather pouch. There were very few travellers on that particular day. As we approached through a small strait on the west, which separated the island from the mainland, I could see there were tall bluffs on the other three sides. Bluffs, that reminded me of the high cliffs of Harbour Grace. Cliffs, that summoned the vision, where once a young couple in love had danced. I sensed my father's presence. There was a small jetty where the ferry was tied up and one of the crew graciously handed us across the drawbridge. A long winding, flagstone path curved its way up from the dock and led to the main entrance. On one side was a dense thicket exuding a deep earthy miasma. On the opposite side of the uneven, rather rugged trail was a tall, grassy glade surrounding a miniature pond, where a pair of white swans lazily circled around the periphery. A nostalgic recollection of what Finn had told me about Swans came to mind.

"Anne, did you not know that white swans pulled the Chariot of Venus through the air, that the feathers of sacred swans were used to cloak heavenly nymphs?"

A serene, unearthly place was this island refuge. Hidden away from the rest of the world it gave me the strange sensation that I had been transported to paradise. In this private oasis, I half expected Venus to appear from behind a tree attended by feathered nymphs or winged fairies.

A branch of the Brigidine sisters operated the hospital. I found that revelation amazing, since I was told that these women were direct descendents of St. Brigid. Had Bridie's soul come to rest here, to protect and look after her son? Did I feel her presence somehow transformed into the body of one of the graceful birds I had just seen floating tranquilly about the tarn?

The nuns scurried about the property in dark habits. They reminded me of the puffins from my homeland. Once inside the front doors of the convalescent hospital, I headed toward the reception area. A round, rosy face smiled up at me from beneath the black armour of God.

"May I be of service?" the face asked.

Once again I told my story. Assuredly, there was a flicker of recognition when I spoke the name Shadrach Pynn.

"If you wait here a moment, I will fetch Mother Superior and convey to her your request." Spoke the flustered, reddened face.

The rotund body waddled off, the hem of her long garment, dusting the floor as she went.

I crossed the room and gazed out the narrow, leaded glass window. The land was beautiful and peaceful. It was easy to understand how the infirmed, diseased and feeble of mind could find solace and strength in these composed surroundings. Directly beneath the balustrade a man bent over in an odd posture was pruning a border of shrubs and bushes. His hand…I noticed something strangely familiar about his hand.

"Miss Pynn"

The deep voice from behind startled me. The woman greeted me with a gentle handshake and beckoned me to join her on a settee, which I noticed had St. Brigid's cross above it on the wall. For a second I doubted if this was happening, if I was in the real world or if it was all just a delusion. Addressing me with a nod of her head and a nervous cough to clear her throat, the Abbess leaned toward me and placed her hand on top of mine. Speaking softly, as though in prayer, she inquired.

"Anne Pynn, I understand that you are the daughter of Shadrach?"

I acceded this to be the truth.

"Your father came here to Deer Island following that fatal fire which took from him the will to live. He reportedly jumped from an upper storey window into a net held by the firemen below. One onlooker said: "He didn't jump, he was pushed. Clad only in a white night shirt he stood at the window surrounded by flames. In one moment he burst into a ball of fire and the glass pane blew out. Appearing from behind a woman in a blue gown pushed him with great force toward the rescue squad on the ground. The woman disappeared back into the blazing building."

Barely breathing, struggling between life and death your father arrived into our hands.

It was only the sister's diligence, constant care and understanding that kept him here on earth. He fought to leave and they opposed. Little by little his condition improved. The war the sister's waged to keep your father amongst us was won. Once he had recuperated from the burns that covered almost the entire one side of his body and it was no longer necessary for him to stay as a patient, he agreed to be kept on as our gardener. His skin remains badly scarred; he has severe contractures, which cause him to lean to his damaged side. His hand on that side looks like a claw and his face is hideously marred. In the seven years that he has been on the island, no one has ever before attempted to visit him. In all this time he has not spoken a single word."

I told the mother superior about my own mother's box and how I had only just recently been able to trace my father's whereabouts to Boston. I told her in great earnestness how I had been compelled to find him, as though some outside force kept moving me toward him. I told her how I didn't believe that he even knew I existed. I told her that I wanted to be united with him so that I could get to know him as my father and he in turn, could get to know his only daughter. The woman, still holding my hand, graciously agreed that we should be brought together.

"We shall have to give considerable consideration to this meeting and arrange it carefully so as not to shock your father unnecessarily. With his fragile composure, it is impossible to predict how the revelation of your existence might affect his inner stability. Your father is working in the garden, I will take you to the library and from there you can observe him for a while without him knowing. You can plan how you are going to tell him who you are. This will give me the opportunity to tell him that he is going to have a visitor. To prepare him for your reunion."

From the library I watched like a thief, stealing glimpses while his head was turned. I looked at the photo. I looked at the man in the garden. They were the same. Except the man in the photo was young, tall and strong.

He was lost.

The man in the garden was older, bent and careworn.

He was found.

This was my father.

CHAPTER 19

1880

CHARLOTTE

The fabric tears
the warp is ripped
the weft parted.
Exposing
truth,
hidden behind
a common thread.

I approached him timidly. He stayed in the garden where the Abbess suggested we meet for the first time. He was sitting on a wooden bench. When I stood in front of him, he raised his eyes and looked up. It was as if I had the photo in my lap and he was staring up at me. I knelt down at his feet, so that I could look up at him, so that I could feel like a child.

"My name is Anne."

No acknowledgement.

"I was named in honour of the flower Queen Anne's Lace."

No response.

"My name is Anne Pynn."

Not even a glimmer of recognition.

"I am the child of Shadrach and Druscilla Pynn. I am your daughter."

My father clutched his throat and looked at me in disbelief.

"It is the truth."

I wanted to take this burned and wounded soul into my arms and never again, never again let him go. But first I had to prove to him, that I was his child; the offspring of his loins, issued forth from his and my mother's undying love for one another. I had to convince him that I was that 'child of lovers—lovers who spawned in fields of grace—that child of favour conceived on the flowers.'

I emptied my haversack and lay before him on the bench: the photos, the journals and the letters. Then taking his twisted talon of a hand, I pried open his fingers and gave him the green ribbon. I spread the immaculate white shawl over his knees.

He did not speak. He beheld each article with reverence. He kissed the green ribbon. A single tear rested in the corner of his eye, then slowly made its way over the cicatrix, mottled mask that had once been the handsome face in the photo.

I recounted how I came to find him. I told him that Bridie had passed on to a better life but before making that final journey, she had revealed to me my parents love for each other and given me my past in a box. I told him about Bridie's will and the hat pin.

He held the picture of my mother toward me with a questioning look.

"My mother died when I was seven. Aunt Charlotte raised me."

Still he did not speak.

I held his hand. We sat there on the bench breathing in and out, in and out, as the day marched forward into twilight.

"Speak to me Papa. Tell me why you left your beloved soul mate. Tell me why you sold the Pynn property that you set out in search of. Tell me why you sent money anonymously through Delilah. Tell me why you never came home."

No words came forth. Yet, I felt the ever so slight paternal pressure as he gripped my hand. I didn't know what to do. I wanted him to speak to me, to answer my questions, to vindicate himself.

Nothing.

As a last resort, I did the unthinkable. I opened the sacred pouch that Bridie had given me. I dipped my fingers inside, where a silken dust feathered the tips with the fine powdery remains of the birth caul. Then I touched them to my father's lips.

He reached for the photo of Gael.

He spoke.

In a voice so soft I could barely hear him he spoke.

"This infant was my daughter. She was born deformed. If you are also my daughter, then you are a miracle."

Moments passed. I beseeched him.

"Don't stop Papa, don't stop talking."

Sighing as though he bore the heaviest of burdens, he continued. He continued to speak for the first time in seven years.

"We were young, Druscilla and I, when our baby was born.

Something was drastically wrong. She died and we buried her as Bridie advised, enclosing the names of three angels written on parchment in her casket. Angel's names hold great mystical and magical power. They are used in prayers, incantations and on amulets. If one believes in them, they can provide protection against the forces of darkness. Carefully we chose three of these divine messengers. Three that we believed would be the best guardians for our little treasure: the angel Afriel, protector of children, Cathetel, the keeper of flowers and finally Satarel, the trustee of hidden elusive and secret knowledge.

Charlotte came to our house as she did to every house where death had crept in a door and stolen away a child, a loved one, a parent or an unsuspecting friend. She had made it her vocation to pray and grieve with the mourners. I never could understand her obsession with the suffering and anguish of others. She thrived on sorrow. I could never fathom the twisted tangle of punishment, penance and forgiveness, which she preached and spat out while moralizing, until that day of our precious Gael's departure.

She called to me."

"Come outside with me Shadrach, I must speak with you."

"I hated moments alone with Charlotte because they inevitably presented her with the opportunity to vent her convictions, which I was never fond of listening to. On that day my guard was down—I went outside with her."

Once again silence lay between us. I implored.

"Tell me, tell me what happened."

My father continued,

"I will tell you now what Charlotte said on that fateful day which changed my life, changed Druscilla's life forever and then you will understand why I left. Always quick to pass judgement, Charlotte seized a moment when I was most vulnerable."

"Shadrach of the fiery furnace you have been punished with the birth and death of your child. It is God's way of seeking retribution for fornicating with your sister."

"I was stunned by this wild, insane accusation. I had known

for a long time who my father was. I had accidentally discovered his identity and Bridie had confirmed my suspicions, telling me the complete story of my conception. Druscilla and I were raised together in the same household as you have undoubtedly found out but we were not brother and sister. We couldn't be, we were not even blood related. I told her emphatically, Charlotte, you are a crazy woman. God has not inflicted punishment on us, nor is he seeking retribution for any sacrilege. You know that. You know that Druscilla and I are not related."

"Oh, but you are. Everyone has been mislead: my father, Brigid, you and Druscilla, everyone. When I was young and innocent and virginal, I was consumed and shamed by a man who I thought was in love with me. I fell from grace, I became with child. If anyone had found out, I would have been branded as a whore and the man's career would have been over. The only person besides myself who knew about my condition was my mother. She devised a plan to keep the pregnancy a secret. She told my father, blind John Soper, that she was going to have a baby. It was a devious, hideous lie. A lie I've lived to regret to this day.

It was easy to hide my pregnancy and relatively simple for my mother to fake hers. However, as you and I both know, the Lord does not tolerate lies nor condone wicked ways. Our guilt in these matters, led to my mother's untimely death immediately upon my child's birth.

Druscilla is really my daughter not my sister.

Believing that his wife had died in childbirth, Blind John took my baby to Bridie to take care of. She was deceived just like everyone else. Your father was Oisin Sweetapple, a revered man of the church. He was the man I thought I was in love with. I thought he was in love with me, but he wasn't. He was in love with Brigid, but she wouldn't have him, she only wanted his seed to make a baby. Druscilla is your sister, there is absolutely no question about it, no denying it."

Shadrach trembled with the telling of this unbelievable tale. His strength from speaking after years of being mute was sapped. I tried to give him solace.

"But you didn't know. You were innocent. My mother, she didn't know either. You cannot be blamed for someone else's misdeeds, nor punished for their sins."

"My love for Druscilla knew no bounds. Her joy was my joy and her torment was my torment. Even with the knowledge of the truth, I could never stop loving her. If I had stayed in Harbour Grace, we would have been together again and again and again. I couldn't take the risk of her conceiving another child like our precious Gael. The pain of knowing what we had done would have devastated her. I didn't tell her the truth. I concealed Charlotte's confession because I could not bear to have Druscilla suffer. The only solution to the whole horrible situation was for me to leave. Druscilla perceived my depression to be as a result of the loss of Gael. So, I used that hopelessness, that despondency, as an excuse. I told her that if I was able to go in search of the Pynn land, that I might not be as disheartened. Because she loved me, she let me go. I guess she did not tell me about you, perhaps because she did not know for certain at that time.

I left, full of sin and remorse. I hoped that by depriving myself of material goods, by offering all of my possessions that I would be forgiven. That is why I sold the Pynn land and sent the money by way of Delilah. It wasn't enough. I deserved more punishment. Engulfed, swallowed up by the hot fires of hell, I believed my life had ended. But death was not the answer; the sisters, my mother's sisters rescued me. They brought me here to exist for the rest of my life, branded, marked with the scars of shame.

Look at you: a vision of perfection. Have you come to take away the scars, to liberate me? Has God finally seen fit to release me from my ignominy?" He asked.

Darkness fell and from the sky a force took hold. I held a corner of the shawl and unknown words uttered forth. An invocation, a charm of Saint Brigid's against a scald.

"Three ladies came from the East,
Two with fire and one with frost.
Out with thee fire, and in with thee, frost."

There they were, the three ladies, dancing in front of us in the dark. The red headed crone, the flaxen haired mother and the maiden, all three released Shadrach Pynn into my keeping.

Then, without hesitation I was able to take this man who was my father into my arms and never again let him go. The wolf that opened the door, the swan that pointed the way and the waiting mermaid never again appeared in my dreams.

CHAPTER 20

1920

HOME TO THE HARBOUR

From the red fire

of adversity,

to the fields

of glorious white,

march the strong.

The mothers

And daughters

The sons

And fathers.

We went home my father and I. I made the arrangements quickly. He said his good byes to the sisters. On our voyage we spent hours talking. I gave him the hat pin and told him about my recurring dream. I told him what a wonderful man his father was with the strength and determination of a wolf. Only in myth would a wolf and swan consort. The likelihood of them uniting would be legendary. He told me that wolves and swans mate for life. I told him about Finn and how we had fallen in love. He smiled for the first time.

It was summer. Three months had elapsed since I had last seen the familiar shores of home. Charlotte, Oisin and Finn each awaited our return.

Each waited with secrets.

We returned with secrets.

Secrets that had been hushed and withheld.

I knew that deep within me grew another secret, the most precious of them all. Could these secrets of the past be laid to rest, so there would be joy rather than fear in our homecoming? We vowed a conspiracy of silence my father and I, to protect our loved ones, those living and those about to be born.

As we approached the Haypook, a hundred white horses galloped forth to greet us. In the distance we could see a blanket of white lace hovering over the rocky banks of Harbour Grace.

EPILOGUE

This is what I discovered. I descend from the families Pynn and Sweetapple. The Sweetapples are distinctly marked with a gene for white hair, like that of my mother Druscilla, my grandfather Oisin and Finn, the father of my child. The red hair of the Pynns has been passed down through many generations. I have it, so did my grandmother Brigid and all her siblings. My daughter Belle has flaming tawny hair with a shock of white growing from her widow's peak.

Given the name Anne, I was most assuredly born with favour and grace. I had a very special relationship with my grandmother and came to honour and respect my grandfather. I am in possession of the shawl, tenderly fashioned by loving hands with a pattern resembling umbelliferae. The mystery of St. Anne's gravidity has never been solved. There is an uncertainty about Belle's origin. There is only one time I could have conceived – in the white room, on the white bed, on the white shawl. I would never pretend to be a Saint but I will not refute the similarities between my life and that of Saint Anne.

My mother Druscilla was the daughter of a minister of the church. Druscilla and Shadrach had a child who died as an infant and seven years later my mother succumbed to a broken heart. Druscilla, the daughter of the high priest Herod Agrippa had a child who perished at the hands of a volcano. The parallel between my mother and this ancient Druscilla cannot be denied. My mother's heart was broken, but in death she continued to reach out her strong arm of love. She danced on a cliff where her arms rose and fell like the gossamer wings of the apias butterfly, lingering gently on a current of air.

My grandmother Brigid was born with a purple birthmark on her face, which disappeared after the birth of her only child Shadrach. Many times she materialized before me as a burst of inspirational light and as a white swan. She appeared to have healing qualities and was adept at writing poetry. She refused to marry the father of her child and told him to look across the valley in order to find a woman who would be good to him and take care of him all the days of his life. Saint Brigid also refused to marry; she disfigured her face so that she would appear ugly and unappealing. Both women had the power to heal. The analogy between Bridie and Saint Brigid also cannot be denied.

The whereabouts of Shadrach Pynn was unknown for twenty years. He was thrown into a fiery furnace for a sin he thought he had committed. I rescued him. I was born with favour and grace. I asked myself then and I ask myself now, is there a connection between my father and Shadrach of the Bible?

It would appear that the flower Umbelliferae has held true to its portent. Brigid conceived, Druscilla conceived and I, Anne conceived while lying on the flowers either real or crocheted. As for the Devils Plague and Mother Die—those stories are left for Belle to recount.

ISBN 1-41205832-5